AF583362

STRANGERS ON COUNTRY

Published by National Library of Australia Publishing
Canberra ACT 2600

ISBN: 9780642279552

The National Library of Australia acknowledges Australia's First Nations Peoples—the First Australians—as the Traditional Owners and Custodians of this land and gives respect to the Elders—past and present—and through them to all Australian Aboriginal and Torres Strait Islander people.

First Nations Peoples are advised that this book contains depictions and names of deceased people, and content that may be considered culturally sensitive. Some words quoted from historical sources, which reflect the author's attitude or that of the period in which the item was written, may be considered inappropriate today.

Editor: Irma Gold
Designer: Amy Cullen
Indexer: Sherrey Quinn
Printed in China through Asia Pacific Offset on FSC®-certified paper

A catalogue record for this book is available from the National Library of Australia.

Find out more about NLA Publishing at library.gov.au/nla-publishing

STRANGERS ON COUNTRY

DAVE HARTLEY & KIRSTY MURRAY
ILLUSTRATED BY DUB LEFFLER

NLA PUBLISHING

STORY LOCATIONS

1. **Narcisse/Anco** lived with the Wanthaala clan of the Nightisland people. They are spiritually connected to land about 120 kilometres north of Princess Charlotte Bay, including seven kilometres of shore, and extending inland about six to ten kilometres and over 40 kilometres out into the sea and the Great Barrier Reef.

2. **Barbara/Giom's ship** was wrecked on Madjii Reef, off Horn Island in the Torres Strait. She lived with the Kaurareg people on Muralug Island, also known as Prince of Wales Island, near the tip of the Cape York Peninsula.

3. **Jemmy's raft** landed on the southern point of Cape Cleveland, a promontory south of present-day Townsville, on the country of the Juru and the Bindal people. Today, this area is home to the town of Bowen.

4. **The Kabi Kabi people's land,** where Jem/Duramboi lived, stretched over 9600 square kilometres, from Caboolture in South East Queensland through to Childers and Hervey Bay in the north.

5. **Mer Island** (also known as Murray Island), is a small island in the eastern section of the Torres Strait and was the home of John/Waki and William/Uass.

CONTENTS

FOREWORD

CHRIS SARRA

There are always two sides to any relationship. Regrettably, Australia's white history books have often only presented the stories of the relationships with Australia's first people from the side of our white colonisers. After all, how could Australia's white colonisers truly explain or provide insight into the perspectives of our first people in those moments of first contact?

For a long time, such insights and perspectives were perhaps not considered worthwhile understanding or knowing about. Over time though, as the relationships between white Australia and our First Australians evolve, we become more cognisant of the importance of understanding and appreciating the perspectives, insights and feelings that exist on both sides of the relationship.

This book is innovative in its efforts to reflect on, and restore life and vibrancy to, both sides of a range of historical relationships. In a way, this lets us unveil a sense of empathy and understanding about the lives of early colonisers and our First Australians. Indeed, such empathy and understanding has an enduring and valid place in relationships between our First Australians and new Australians, even today.

One thing made clear by the work of these two innovative authors is that today—as well as at those points of first contact many, many years ago—positive and loving relationships are always possible when we let ourselves be connected by our humanity.

May all who read this work be inspired to contemplate the perspectives, insights and feelings on both sides of any complex relationship, and may all be inspired to be connected by our humanity.

Chris Sarra is the Executive Chair of the Stronger Smarter Institute.

INTRODUCTION

DAVE HARTLEY AND KIRSTY MURRAY

Imagine being an Aboriginal or Torres Strait Islander person 200 years ago. Mysterious people with white skin were arriving on the land that your people had lived on for tens of thousands of years. These people began to kill your people, take your land, claim it as their own and then farm it with new crops and odd-looking animals.

Now, imagine if one of these strangers washed up on the shore from an overnight shipwreck. What would you do? Take them in? Feed them? Care for them as one of your own family members?

To Aboriginal and Torres Strait Islander people, the first castaways and runaway convicts that arrived in their homes must have appeared pretty scary. The strangers didn't speak their language and didn't understand their ways, but they were desperately in need of refuge. Despite their fears, the Indigenous hosts often treated the lost strangers with kindness, taking pity on them and giving them food and shelter.

The stories in this book are based on true stories that are documented in historical records. In working together, we imagined the stories from both the Indigenous and the European points of view. Unfortunately, all the different sources that we drew upon were written only by white people, so we thought very carefully, and had long discussions, about how to tell the stories from both sides. We used both our heads and our hearts to recreate the past.

Each story in this book is told through two historical fiction narratives. The first is from the point of view of an Indigenous person who befriends the stranger in their land. The second is from the point of view of the castaway or convict who is given refuge. At the end of each chapter, there is a section of facts and information. Dave is a proud descendant of the Barunggam people of Queensland, so he wrote the stories from the point of view of the Indigenous people. Kirsty is descended from convicts and early immigrants so she imagined what it was like to be one of the castaways or convicts. Then we collaborated to make the facts and stories thread together. At all times, we wrote within the boundaries of the documented information available to us.

Too often Australian history is told only from the point of view of the Europeans who sailed here from across the world, and not through the eyes of the First Australians who lived here and loved this ancient land for countless centuries. In writing this book, we hope to help you, our reader, think about how all Australians today can learn from traditional Indigenous ways of thinking and doing. When we listen to and understand others, work with people, instead of doing things to people, then we can all begin to adopt the wise ways of the past.

This book was inspired by and based on Living with the Locals: Early Europeans' Experience of Indigenous Life *by John Maynard and Victoria K. Haskins and we would like to thank both the authors for their support and encouragement.*

1 THE NIGHT-ISLAND PEOPLE AND THE CABIN BOY

PRINCESS CHARLOTTE BAY, QUEENSLAND, 1858–1875

SASSY

ONE AFTERNOON JUST ON DUSK, WHEN THE DUGONG WERE FEEDING IN THE GRASS BEDS CLOSE TO THE SHORELINE, THERE CAME A SHOUT FROM THE BEACH.

'Sassy! Move those skinny legs of yours and get over here. Look what Uncle Maademan's caught.'

What was it this time? Uncle Maademan was one of our best hunters. He's got a big fat turtle for dinner, I thought. But I was wrong, very wrong.

I raced out of my hut like an emu and headed for the beach. By the time I got there, our whole village was beginning to crowd around Uncle and one of the other hunters, but when they saw Uncle's catch, many of the women and children screamed in fright, running for the safety of the trees.

'Let me see!' I shouted, jumping up to look over the men's shoulders, trying to be brave. But as usual no one was interested in me.

As the men started to talk excitedly about Uncle Maademan's amazing treasure, some of the women began cautiously returning to the circle. Taking a closer look at what Uncle had found, they laughed like kookaburras.

'Shame! I'm so embarrassed,' giggled one of my aunties.

Some of the men made fun of the women for being so scared in the first place. I started climbing a tree to get a better look.

'Where did you find it?' asked one of our Elders.

'Under the trees near the dugong grounds,' said Uncle.

I climbed onto a thick branch and pushed a switch of leaves away. Finally I could see Uncle's discovery.

A thin white child lay on the beach, with skin as fair as the coral sand. The stranger looked sick and scared and the soles of its feet were cut and bleeding. The women started tending the wounds. As they rinsed the child's feet in fresh water, there was a cry of pain. Startled, the crowd jumped back.

'It makes noises like us,' said the Elder.

As the women continued to clean the wounds, the Elder inspected the child by gripping its hands and counting its fingers.

'Same as us!' our Elder announced.

The child looked around nervously with eyes as wide as two full moons.

'Is it a boy or a girl?' asked a man.

The Elder checked. 'Definitely a boy,' he said seriously.

Everyone was surprised that the young person in front of them could be a boy, especially because of his strange clothes and hair.

'What will we do with him?' asked an Elder.

Uncle Maademan stepped forward and put his spear in the sand. 'I found him, so I will adopt him as my son,' he said calmly.

Everyone became excited again. The Elders next to the boy whispered to each other.

'If he is your son, what will be his name?' asked one of them.

The crowd hushed and waited for Uncle to answer.

'I will call him Anco,' announced Uncle Maademan.

Anco and I became cousins and when his wounds healed, I was given the important job of showing him our country. We explored the bushland and I proudly showed him how to take care near the swamp, especially when the crocodiles were nesting. Anco quickly learned our language and wanted to become a hunter, just like me and the other boys. We had to be patient and wait until we had come of age.

One day when we were collecting wood for the fire, some of the older kids began teasing Anco.

'Look at his pale skin,' they said. 'He's not your cousin, Sassy. He's a ghost.'

They ran off when Uncle Maademan told them to stop, but the teasing continued.

As we became men and were given permission to hunt, some of our people became jealous of Anco because he was one of our best spear-makers.

'You're so good, it's like you were born on country,' I would say to him after he had finished attaching a sharp iron spike to the end of a spear. Anco would smile and give the best spears to Maademan.

'Here, Father, this is for you,' he would say.

When the young men needed to be punished for doing something wrong, Uncle never hit Anco. The only time Anco was punished was when he ate the special fish that was reserved for the old people. No one was ever allowed to eat that fish except for them. Anco never ate that fish again.

Anco and I were initiated together, fought together, sang together, and hunted side by side. As our bodies matured, so did the way we saw the world. The white boy that Anco once was had become a man of the Nightisland people.

One day, white men arrived in a big wooden canoe. They offered our people knives, jewellery, and tobacco and pipes for smoking. Maademan told Anco to go with them to their ship and then swim back to us when he had received the gifts.

Just as he would follow Maademan's instructions when he was a boy, Anco showed the same respect as a man. Maademan watched proudly as Anco—who now bore the initiation scars of manhood—entered the white man's canoe.

But that was the last time we saw him. The men stole Anco and when they reached the ship they sailed away forever.

Maademan was sad until the day he passed. I was too. I had lost my cousin and best friend. I will always remember him standing at the front of our boat, gliding through the warm blue waters of our hunting grounds. Anco would stand proudly, spear in hand, ready to catch dinner and share it with the people who loved him the most—his family.

NARCISSE PELLETIER/ANCO

WE WERE ALL DYING OF THIRST. I TRIED TO KEEP UP WITH THE MEN BUT EACH STEP WAS LIKE WALKING ON KNIVES.

My feet were slashed to pieces, torn by sharp coral when I had helped drag our longboat to shore. Ahead of me I could see Captain Pinard and the crew scooping up handfuls of fresh water and laughing with relief. By the time I caught up, the waterhole was dry.

I fell to my knees and raked my fingers through the damp soil. 'You've left me nothing!'

'Be patient, boy,' said Captain Pinard. 'The waterhole will refill. You only need to wait.'

I lay on the hot ground clutching my tin cup, longing for more water to seep up through the earth. The Captain and his men turned away from me.

'Where are you going?' I called after them.

'To the beach,' replied the Captain, his voice faint as he disappeared into the bush. 'Don't worry, Narcisse, we'll come back for you.'

Hours passed and the waterhole only grew drier. No one returned. As I lay there alone, I thought of my *mère* and *père* and my little brothers at home in France. I listened to the distant sound of the sea lapping against the beach and almost choked on my misery.

Eventually, I struggled to my feet and retraced my steps to the beach. Standing at the water's edge, I scanned the horizon.

The longboat, the Captain and all the crew were gone. They had tricked me. They had drunk the last of the water, lied about the waterhole refilling, and abandoned me to my fate.

I wandered for hours, moving painfully along the shore and then into the tropical forest. By the next day, I was so weak from hunger and thirst that I was speechless when I came across three naked black women. The women took one look at me and ran screaming into the scrub. A moment later, two Aboriginal hunters appeared, their spears raised and pointed straight at my heart.

I didn't want to die but I was too weak to run or hide. I fell to my knees. 'Please,' I whispered. 'Please don't kill me.'

Slowly, I held out my tin cup, praying they would accept it and spare me.

The men lowered their spears, took the cup and began to talk to each other in a strange, garbled language. I had no idea what they were saying but I knew I had pleased them. I thought I had nothing left to give until I remembered my white handkerchief. I reached into my pocket, drew it out, and offered it up to the black men.

The tallest man smiled, and as our eyes met it was as if a pact was forged between us. He reached down and hooked his hand under my arm, helping me to my feet.

They took me to their camp, gave me food and drink and a warm place by their camp fire. They spoke gently to me, and even though I couldn't understand a word, I knew they meant me no harm.

When I woke the next morning, the camp was empty. I didn't want to cry. I was 14 years old. I had been at sea for two years. I had sailed across the world and survived a shipwreck. But I didn't want to die alone on this godforsaken island.

When I saw the natives returning, I cried with relief. They had gathered breakfast for me; small plums that they called *muungkal*. Though the fruit was as sweet and delicious as fresh dates, I couldn't stop crying.

'*Merci, merci beaucoup, merci*,' I said, and I prayed my new friends would never abandon me.

In my first few seasons living with the Nightisland people, I had much to learn. Even when I understood their language, I didn't always understand their ways, and my habits were often strange to them.

One morning, when I was washing my face and hands, a group of children stood pointing and laughing at me, as if I was playing a crazy game. Sassy heard their laughter and came down to the water's edge to shoo the children away.

'Anco,' he said, shaking his head. 'What are you trying to do? Scrub that white skin away so you can be proper black again?'

'No,' I said, smiling. 'Just washing. But thank you for stopping the children from teasing me.'

I looked up at Sassy with gratitude. 'You're always saving me. I thought Father said it was only the old people's fish that we aren't allowed to eat. I didn't think anyone would mind if I took some turtle meat from yesterday's hunt.'

'You have to learn, cousin. There are rules about how we share.'

I took a deep breath and sighed. 'I know that now and it won't happen again. But I was glad you were there yesterday. That angry fellow would have put a spear in me if you hadn't stopped him.'

Sassy slapped me on the shoulder. 'I could never let anything happen to you, cousin. You are Uncle Maademan's favourite. Mine too!'

I nodded and we ran back to camp together to collect our fishing spears.

As the seasons became years, my old life in France became a dream. My cousin Sassy would laugh when I tried to tell him of that other world. I had left France as a boy but I became a man hunting and fishing on the Cape York Peninsula.

Sometimes I'd look at Sassy and be aware of my strangeness. My skin was a light red-brown compared to his rich dark skin, but when I stood on the front of our canoe, watching the sparkling waters as we hunted for dugong, I was glad to belong to the Nightisland people.

Usually when ships approached, I stayed well away. But one day, I was on the beach with Sassy when a longboat crewed by a handful of men landed on our island. The sailors offered us tobacco, pipes, a knife and a necklace, but I didn't like the way they looked at me, eating me up with their eyes.

The sailors returned later in the day with even more dazzling gifts. They pointed at the fabrics and tools and at their distant ship, and then they pointed at me.

'I think they're trying to say they'll give us more of these things if you go to their ship to collect them,' said my father, Maademan.

'I don't trust them,' I said.

Maademan shook his head. 'Don't be afraid. If there is any sign of trouble, I want you to dive over the edge and swim straight back to us. Even if you come back empty-handed, at least you will have tried.'

'As you wish, Father.'

Reluctantly, I climbed into the longboat. The sailors offered me biscuits that I cautiously accepted. My heart began to race when I realised that they had muskets hidden in the boat. As they rowed away from the shore, they raised their guns and pointed them at me.

I heard my father cry out, 'Anco, come back! Now!'

But it was too late. The sailors aimed their muskets at my family and friends on the beach, and then fired over their heads. Petrified, I gripped the wooden seat, afraid to move for fear they would shoot me, or worse still take proper aim at my family and kill them all.

By the time we reached the ship, I knew I was being kidnapped. On board, white men crowded around me, prattling in a foreign tongue. Even if they had spoken French, I'm not sure I would have understood them. It had been so long since I'd heard the language of my birthplace.

I turned away, gazing back at the beach where my father and my people cried out for me. I had been kidnapped, stolen from the people who had loved me as their own son for 17 years.

THE FACTS

SASSY AND NARCISSE PELLETIER/ANCO

Who was Narcisse Pelletier before he became Anco?

Narcisse Pelletier/Anco was born in 1844 in the seaport of Saint-Gilles-Sur-Vie near Bordeaux in France. At the age of 12, he took his first job as a cabin boy. In 1858, the ship he was working on, the *Saint Paul*, was wrecked south of New Guinea. Narcisse/Anco, Captain Pinard and a handful of sailors, sailed a longboat across the Coral Sea to Australia, where 14-year-old Narcisse/Anco was abandoned by his shipmates.

The captain and his men sailed on in search of a British settlement. A few days later, their boat was taken from them and they spent several days with the Wuthathi Aboriginal people before being rescued by British sailors and taken to Nouméa, New Caledonia. From there, Pinard and his men eventually returned to France. Pinard claimed he 'lost' Narcisse/Anco, though there is no doubt that he abandoned the boy to his fate.

Who was Sassy?

Sassy was a member of the Wanthaala clan of the Uutaalnganu language group, known today as the Nightisland people. Along with two other groups, the Uutaalnganu were known as Pama Malngkana—the people of the sand beach. They lived on Northeast Cape York Peninsula, where Narcisse/Anco was rescued by Sassy's family. Narcisse/Anco told his story to a French-speaking lieutenant on the ship that took him to Sydney and then, when he returned to France, to a French writer called Constant Merland, who published a book about him called *Seventeen Years with the Savages: The Adventures of Narcisse Pelletier*. Narcisse/Anco frequently mentioned Sassy and his Aboriginal father, Maademan, when talking of his time with the Nightisland people.

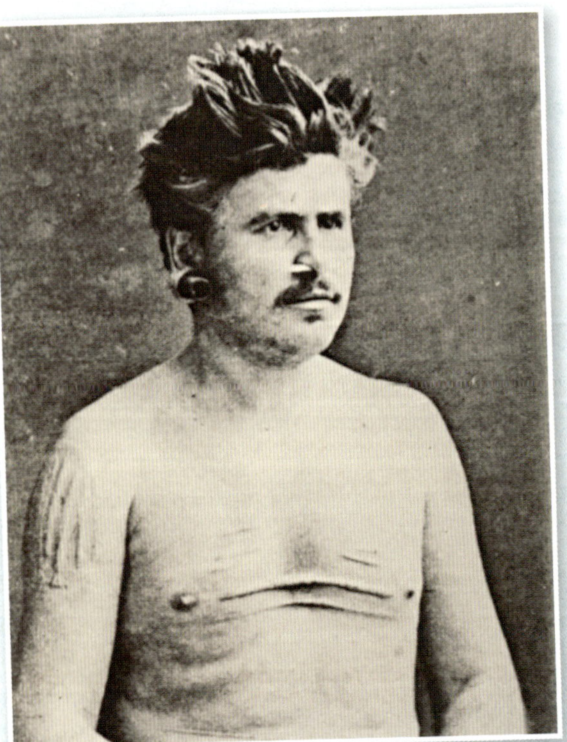

Narcisse/Anco had ritual markings on his chest and arms. The cuts were made using broken glass and carefully filled with sand to make raised scars. This procedure is called 'scarification' and the marks are called 'cicatrices'. Narcisse/Anco had pierced ears and wore a thick circle of wood in the lobe of his right ear. He also wore a piece of elongated shell through the septum of his nose.

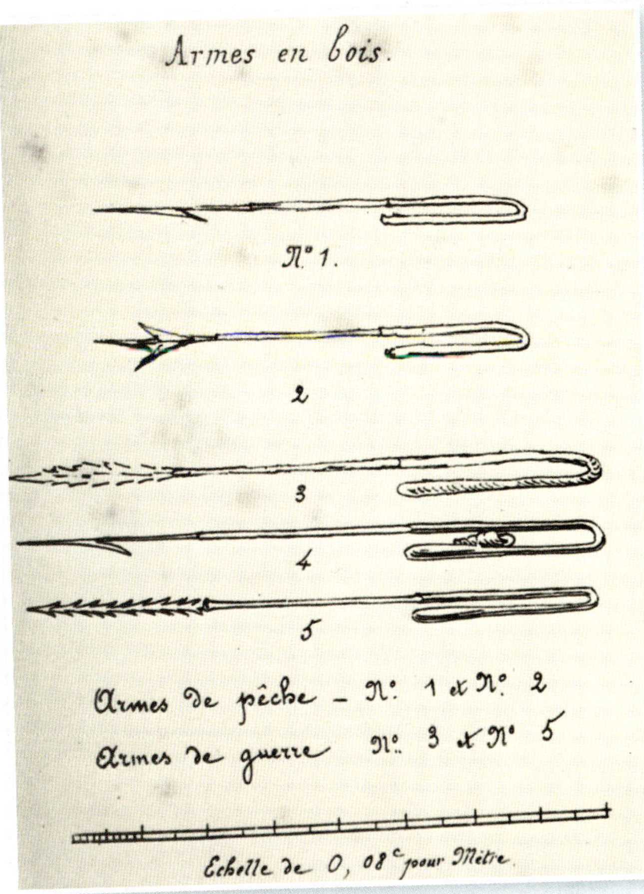

Specialised fishing spears. Narcisse/Anco and Sassy would have used similar weapons to catch fish, turtles and dugong. They did not use nets, lines or baits but only special fishing spears with splayed and barbed hooks to catch fish, and iron-pronged harpoons for hunting dugong.

Although the Nightisland people originally made their tools and weapons from emu and kangaroo bone and sharpened shells, by the time Narcisse/Anco came to live with them they were using glass and iron from shipwrecks.

Who was Narcisse/Anco's Aboriginal family?

Maademan, Sassy and Narcisse/Anco belonged to the Pama Malngkana, a community which is made up of three separate groups, each with their own language: the Kuuku Ya'u, the Uutaalnganu and the Umpila. Narcisse/Anco learned to speak the Uutaalnganu language fluently.

Narcisse/Anco's Aboriginal family, the Wanthaala clan, consisted of around 30 people who belonged to the Uutaalnganu language group. They are also called Nightisland people by other Aboriginal people.

How many years did Narcisse/Anco live with the locals?

Narcisse/Anco spent 17 years with the Nightisland people, from 1858 to 1875. He was a boy of 14 years of age when he arrived on the Cape York Peninsula. By the time he returned to France he was a 32-year-old man.

What did they eat?

The Nightisland people loved to hunt and fish. They were excellent seafarers. The land provided an endless supply of fresh vegetables and fruits, including coconuts, native gooseberries and native plums. The people gathered shellfish from the beaches and reefs and fished and hunted from canoes. There were also crocodiles, snakes, lizards and giant amethystine (or scrub) pythons to hunt and eat, as well as many birds, including ducks, parrots, cockatoos, hens, doves, pigeons, emus and cassowaries.

THE FACTS

SASSY AND
NARCISSE PELLETIER/ANCO

How did they live?

The Pama Malngkana had strict laws about everything from hunting to family obligations and marriage. Murder was punishable by death.

The Pama Malngkana held many ceremonies and Narcisse/Anco learned to sing their songs and perform dances. He also took part in staged battles between different groups, a little like medieval tournaments. Groups of warriors would fight to practise their skills.

When Narcisse/Anco was interviewed in Sydney and France he was very careful not to reveal any secrets or knowledge that was sacred to his Aboriginal family. When questioned, it was obvious he knew more than he was willing to share.

Why did Narcisse/Anco leave?

In April 1875, the crew aboard an English pearling lugger, the *John Bell*, saw Narcisse/Anco with his family and thought they should rescue him because they realised he was a white man. Narcisse/Anco believed he was kidnapped. He was taken first to the settlement at Somerset in Queensland, where he was kept tied up to stop him escaping. He spent time sitting on a fence, bewildered and miserable. He spoke no English and few people spoke French. Then he was taken to Sydney, where he spent a month, before sailing back to France.

Somerset in Cape York, Queensland.

II

Narcisse Pierre Pelletier
Le 11 juillette 1875

Mon cher Père et Ma cher mère et mon frère, je vous écrie une autre foi. je vous enbarse De tout Mon cœur. si vous êtes vivant. je suis arrivé à nouméa le consule de sydney Ma envoyez. je suis A bord d'un navire De guerre. je partirait Dans un mois à bord Du autre navire qui est venu il y a trois Jour, je me Porte Bien j'ai toujour mal à la gambe Droite. il y à Bien longtemps que j'ai mal, j'avait et Bien De la misère avec eux. il mon on Poisonnez la gambe. Mais seulement je me Porte Bien.

Je vous dit Bonjour
Narcisse Pierre Pelletier

Narcisse/Anco quickly regained his own language, French, after he left northern Australia. In this letter sent to his parents from Sydney, he wrote: 'I embrace you with all my heart if you are still alive.'

Narcisse/Anco's French family were bewildered by his appearance and his new spiritual beliefs. They found him so alarming that they even called in the Catholic priest to exorcise whatever spirit possessed him.

What happened when Narcisse/Anco returned to France?

Narcisse/Anco's French family were shocked and amazed by the news of his survival. His mother had worn black mourning clothes ever since his disappearance. When he finally reached his home, the townspeople staged a huge bonfire to celebrate. Narcisse/Anco lit the fire and everyone cheered 'Long Live Pelletier'. But Narcisse/Anco was almost indifferent to the celebrations. The warm welcome cooled. Some people began to call him *'le sauvage'* (the savage) for his strange ways.

Eventually he married but he had no children. A quiet, lonely man, he worked at the harbour of Saint-Nazaire and died 18 years later at the age of 50. He spent his last years staring out over the dark waters of the harbour, perhaps thinking of his life on the shores of Cape York Peninsula.

What happened to the people who cared for Narcisse/Anco?

Although the Pama Malngkana had seen white people occasionally before they met Narcisse Pelletier, there were few European settlements in North Queensland in the 1850s. Forty-three tribal nations lived on the Cape York Peninsula at the time of the European invasion. Many Aboriginal and Torres Strait Islander people were murdered by the new settlers or died of diseases introduced from Europe, but there is still a strong and rich Indigenous culture on the Cape York Peninsula and throughout the Torres Strait Islands. Ten languages are still spoken in the region, as well as many local dialects. Some accounts of Anco's time with the Nightisland people report his name as 'Amglo' but 'Anco' sounds much more like an Uutaalnganu word.

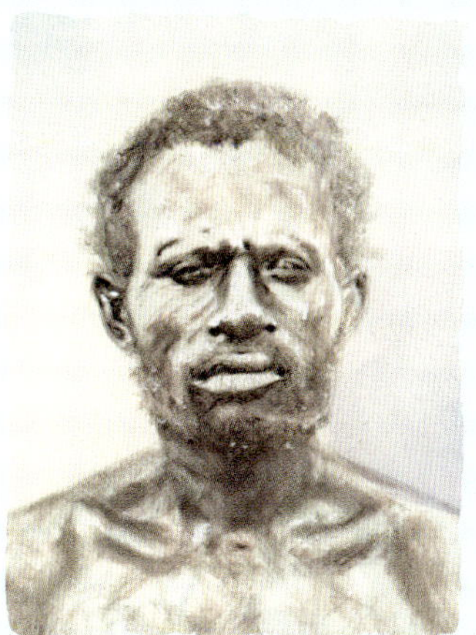

THE KAURAREG ISLANDERS AND THE GHOST GIRL

TORRES STRAIT, 1844–1849

TOMAGUGU

THE SCARS ON MY FOREARM ITCHED. THEY ALWAYS DID WHEN TROUBLE WAS BREWING. LAST YEAR IT HAPPENED ONLY SECONDS BEFORE A SHARK NEARLY CAPSIZED THE BOAT.

Recently someone from our neighbouring tribe mistook me for a thief and the scars tingled minutes before a spear whizzed past my head.

'I'm sorry, Tomagugu,' the tribesman cried. 'Someone has been stealing our fishing nets and they look like you.'

I pulled his spear from the tree trunk and broke it over my knee. My wife, Sibi, ran to my side.

'My husband may be from the mainland but you will treat him as one of us,' she said.

'What can I do to say sorry?' the man pleaded.

'Try throwing your spears at the right people,' I said, handing him the two broken pieces of wood.

On the day of the storm I was out on the boat. My scars were irritating me more than sharing my bed with an echidna. It wasn't long before I found out why.

'Look, there's someone in the water,' yelled Boroto.

'More than one,' added Alikia, standing at the head of the boat, pointing at the struggling souls.

We all stood and waved, calling out to the people to hold fast until we could reach them.

As soon as the storm had eased a little, I threw the last turtle into the canoe and we paddled hard into the wind towards the pieces of boat that had been smashed on the reef.

'Where are they?' Boroto shouted. He looked around at the foaming white water, our canoe bobbing up and down. The wind had slowed. A white girl clinging to a long piece of timber rose to the surface.

When we lifted her into the canoe, her skin was almost pale blue and she was weak.

'Is it a spirit?' asked Alikia.

'Maybe,' I said. 'We must show the Elders.'

The other people had disappeared. They had gone to sleep forever, deep under the water.

Pequi was a respected Elder of the Kaurareg people. Sibi and I enjoyed Pequi's company so much that it was always hard to return home to the mainland after we'd visited the Kaurareg. Boroto, Alikia and I showed Pequi the strange girl who we had pulled from the water.

Pequi held her face and looked at it closely. 'Gieowma!' he cried.

Gieowma was his daughter. We had always called her Giom for short. She had also gone to sleep under the water many moons ago.

'She has Gieowma's eyes,' said Pequi. 'It is her!'

Our people ran up and touched her. They were amazed that the spirit of Pequi's daughter had risen from the sea. It was a day of celebration for everyone in the Kaurareg.

After all those years of being asleep, Giom had forgotten our language and had to be taught again. Everyone was kind to her, but some of the women felt a bit jealous of the attention she was given. Some of them were also mad that Giom had forgotten her manners, just like she had forgotten her language.

One day I returned from the reef with a fat turtle for dinner. Before I could even think about how sweet this turtle would taste after being slow-cooked on the fire, or how my family would feast happily, the scars on my arm began itching. Slowly at first, but then they got stronger until they were a constant prickly sensation. When I heard the women shouting, it made sense.

'You've forgotten our ways, Giom,' growled Yuri, another Kaurareg woman. 'Why don't you invite me to use your oven after you've cooked turtle eggs?'

I'd never seen Yuri so angry. She picked up a turtle shell and threw it at Giom. People started to gather.

'Stop it!' cried Giom.

She filled the turtle shell with water and threw it in Yuri's face. Then she leapt at her, pulling Yuri by the hair and punching her.

Old Pequi heard the commotion and ran towards Yuri with his hunting knife.

'No, Uncle! Stop!' Boroto caught Pequi and held him back.

Boroto was no stranger to a fight. He was one of the bravest and fiercest of the Kaurareg but he did not like seeing his own people at war, especially old Pequi.

When the women finished fighting, Boroto released Pequi from his grasp. As Pequi shrugged him off, he was shaking.

'My daughter has only just come back to me,' he cried to Yuri. 'Why must you treat her like this?'

Racked with guilt for offending old Pequi, Yuri fled into the trees and stayed there. The aunties said she was sulking, but two whole days and nights is a long time to sulk. When she returned, both hungry and tired, I was the first one she spoke to.

'You're clever, Tomagugu. How can I make peace with Pequi?' she asked.

I looked at the scars on my arm. They weren't itching. This was a good sign. I pointed in the direction of Sibi.

'Ask her,' I said. 'She understands women better than me.' I laughed.

Yuri sat with Sibi and drank tea. It was the first thing to pass through Yuri's lips in two days, and she slurped noisily.

'Just walk with Giom,' Sibi said wisely. 'That's what I do with Tomagugu after we fight. Pequi will forgive you if you do this.'

Yuri smiled and finished her tea. 'Thank you,' she said.

Next time Sibi and I came to visit from the mainland, I saw Giom and Yuri digging yams together. Their fighting was over.

It was an afternoon much like the one when Giom and Yuri had their big fight when I arrived among the Kaurareg with another fat turtle for dinner. Sibi saw me coming—she stopped preparing the oven and rushed towards me, speaking in whispers.

'She wants to go!' said Sibi.

I pulled the turtle from my back and placed it at our feet. Sibi was so distracted that she didn't even notice how big the turtle was.

'Who wants to go where?' I asked, impatiently.

Sibi glared at me, and understanding cut through me like a cold wind from the south.

'It's Giom! The women have heard her calling out to the white men's boats as they sail past,' Sibi explained. 'She cries herself to sleep when they don't stop for her.'

I thought long and hard about this while feeling about in my bag for sharp stones to cut the turtle.

'Pequi will be heartbroken,' I said.

I thought about whether or not to tell him. There were secrets we had kept from him, worried that Giom would break his heart again.

Once, Badu Island men tried to take Giom away, but Alikia and I wouldn't let them, telling them that Giom was scared and did not want to travel with them. Worse, one day Giom tried to leave with Islanders visiting from the north. Boroto and I caught her just before she hopped into their canoe.

'I would sooner kill you than let you go with these people,' yelled Boroto.

Giom became fearful and upset at his strong words.

'Pequi needs you,' I reminded Giom. 'You're family.'

The day after the fat turtle dinner, Giom approached me and Sibi. The familiar itch tingled lightly on my forearm.

'Can we sit?' Giom asked, her eyes watering.

Sibi lowered herself to the ground and so did I. Giom did the same and rested her head on my wife's shoulder.

'Your own people. You miss them greatly,' I said, seeing the desperation in Giom's eyes.

'You want to be with them, don't you?' asked Sibi, putting her arm around Giom.

Giom didn't reply through words, only tears. At that moment, Pequi walked past, inspecting the turtle first, and then Giom. Pequi's silence was one of understanding. From that day forward, we often sat with Giom by the water, looking out towards the white men's boats.

'Our time with you is growing shorter,' I said, handing her a beautiful fan shell.

Giom held it in her fingertips. 'If I can shake their hands,' she said, 'I'm sure they'll take me home.'

Sibi threw me a worried look. 'Are you sure this is how you want to live?' she asked Giom. 'As a white person?'

'It is who I am,' answered Giom.

Sibi rubbed Giom's arm lightly. 'Then Tomagugu shall speak to Pequi.'

I gulped and my arm began to itch.

Pequi's heartbreak began on the day that the next big boat sailed up to our islands. As I had promised, I found a place for Giom in a canoe that was taking many of the Kaurareg to see the white men. Giom sat beside Sibi, her eyes bright with excitement.

We came across the sailors at the entrance to one of our hunting grounds. The men were covered in strange clothes and held equally strange weapons. They hunted the same birds as us, but were noisy and clumsy, shouting and stomping through the bushes.

Sibi and I stood either side of Giom, expecting the men to stop and stare at the white girl in our care. But they walked straight past us, not even surprised that one of their own people had been living among us.

Giom was truly one of the Kaurareg now. I called out to the white men, trying to explain that we had found one of their own people in the water and saved her, but Giom pushed me aside. She yelled at them in her language and they turned around and stared at her. One of the men came close and they spoke for a good while. He reached out and held her hand. She walked with him and boarded their big boat.

For many days and nights, Giom stayed on that boat and began to wear their clothes and eat their food. She seemed happier. Sibi and I would visit her, but not with Boroto. He was wild that Giom had left us. He couldn't understand why she would want to leave the Kaurareg.

Other canoes with Kaurareg people also sailed out to visit Giom. They wanted her to come back, but she stayed on that boat until the day it sailed away. Pequi was going to lose his daughter again, but the woman who was torn between two worlds had finally made her decision.

As she disappeared over the horizon, I understood something. Just like the tides that came in and went out, so too did Giom. She was in control of her own destiny and Giom was a tide that would never come back in.

BARBARA THOMPSON/GIOM

HUGE WAVES CRASHED AGAINST OUR BOAT. I TRIED TO SCREAM FOR HELP BUT MY MOUTH FILLED WITH SEAWATER AND THE OCEAN SUCKED AT MY CLOTHES, DRAGGING ME UNDER.

As our cutter smashed to pieces on the reef, I clung to the wreckage, fighting for my life. I saw my husband, Will, trying to swim to shore, but he was too weak to stay the distance. Perhaps Will Thompson had always been weak. I thought he would save me but he couldn't even save himself.

Will was always talking me into things I shouldn't do. He told me if I ran away from home with him, we'd have a grand life. He told me if we sailed up north to rescue oil from a sunken shipwreck, we'd be rich. He was a grown man and I was only 12 years old. Of course, I'd believed him. But as I watched him drown, I knew Will Thompson would never again tell me another story or another lie.

I was alone in the wild sea, praying to God to save me, when through the sea spray I saw movement. Three black men were waving at me from an island. I heard their voices, calling out, '*Toomah*, *toomah*, bye and bye,' encouraging me to hold fast.

When the storm died down, the natives paddled out to rescue me. They took me from the water and then bundled me gently into their canoe. I trembled with fear but they spoke softly and took me to their island where they fed me turtle soup that they had boiled in a large shell. It was hot and delicious and I wanted to cry with relief as I sipped it. I smiled up at the black men by way of thanks.

The seasons turned and I lost track of how many years I lived with the Kaurareg. When I was rescued from the raging sea I had imagined myself a grown-up. But on Muralug Island, I grew tall and strong. My skin became tanned and my hair grew thick and curly. I changed from a girl to a full-grown woman. Despite this my new father, Pequi, treated me like a child. He called me Giom, never Barbara or Mrs Thompson, and his eyes shone with happiness whenever he saw me. The Kaurareg thought of white people as ghosts because they were not born on country and so had no spirit that connected them to the land. When Pequi gave me the name of his own daughter who had drowned, I was less of a ghost girl and could take her place in the community. Yet I couldn't stop thinking of my old life, my blood kin and the world that was lost to me.

One time, after I had missed the chance of meeting sailors who had visited our island, old Gameema found me weeping on the banks of the waterhole. She put her arms around me and comforted me.

'They probably wouldn't want me anymore,' I cried in despair. 'My skin is too black now, my hair too wild.'

Gameema cooed and fussed over me and led me back to camp. Even though she offered me sweet yams, I couldn't eat for two days. I was sick with grief and longing.

Then one bright, clear morning I saw Tomagugu and his wife, Sibi, land their canoe on the beach. They often came over from the mainland to visit me. Though Tomagugu was from the mainland, Sibi's family were Kaurareg and I had entrusted both of them with my feelings, telling them how much I longed to return to my people.

'Sibi, Tomagugu,' I called, as I ran along the white sands to meet them. 'Have you heard about the new ghost ship?'

'Yes, and we've come to help you,' said Tomagugu.

'Are you sure the Kaurareg will let me go?' I asked. 'They treat me like I'm their darling pet. I can't make anyone believe that I want to go back to live among the *marki*. They don't understand why anyone would want to live with ghost people.'

Sibi frowned and shook her head. She had always found it hard to accept that I would want to leave the islands. But Tomagugu smiled. 'Don't you mind them. I always said that one day you'd go back to your own people, Giom. I've spoken with Pequi and explained. We'll take you to the white men and make sure you're safe.'

I was stunned. I'd been crying all night about yet another ship passing me by. I smiled up at Tomagugu. 'Ever since you saved me, you've known my heart. If it wasn't for you, I might have lost hope.'

Tomagugu made sure I was given a place in the last canoe that would cross the bay to find the white men. Many of the Kaurareg wanted to trade with the sailors, but I wanted so much more. I could barely contain my excitement when I saw the HMS *Rattlesnake* moored across the bay.

Tomagugu and Sibi led me through the bush, following the sound of gunfire and men speaking English. When we found the hunting party of white men, we watched as they loaded their guns and shot a brace of birds. My heart began to pound. I stood staring at the sailors, waiting for them to cry out in surprise at the sight of me, but they walked straight past, barely glancing my way!

In panic, I called out: 'I am a white woman! Why do you leave me?'

The men stopped and turned to stare. Only then, I realised I was naked. Why had I left my grass skirt behind? How could I forget to be ashamed?

As I hung my head, Tomagugu stepped forward, telling them in his own talk how he had taken me up out of the water, as if I couldn't understand the questions the sailors were firing at me.

I took a breath and snapped at Tomagugu. 'Brother, hold your tongue. I know what they are saying.'

When I opened my mouth to speak again, English and Kaurareg words swirled inside my head and I was tongue-tied. Tears tumbled down my cheeks.

'So where are you from, girlie?' asked a sailor.

'I'm a Scottish girl and my mother and father are in Sydney,' I said slowly. 'This man is like a brother to me and he saved me when I was shipwrecked but I want to go back to my ma and pa.'

'Scott, Scott, come here!' called the sailor.

The man called Scott was from Scotland, like me, and his accent was warm and familiar.

'Do not cry, little lass,' he said.

He took me by the hand, so brave like, so gentle, and led me to a nearby waterhole. He washed me and combed my hair and dressed me in two shirts, one below as a petticoat, the other over my shoulders.

On board the big ship, HMS *Rattlesnake*, I was given tea and meat and sweet apple pie. The food tasted as strange to me as the sound of the English language. I shut my eyes and a tear trickled down my cheek.

'Do you want to go back to the blacks, or do you want to come away with us to Sydney?' asked the captain, impatiently.

I wished someone else would decide for me. I thought of old Pequi and how broken-hearted he would be to lose his daughter again. I thought of my real father in Sydney. I didn't know if he had been released from prison yet, or what had become of my family, but there had to be someone who would be glad to see me.

'Sir, I am a Christian, and would rather go back to my friends,' I replied. It seemed like the right thing to say, even though I wasn't sure if any of my Sydney friends would even remember me.

THE KAURAREG ISLANDERS AND THE GHOST GIRL

I was nine weeks aboard the *Rattlesnake*, waiting for the sailors to finish their visits to the islands. Every day my Kaurareg friends paddled out in canoes to visit me.

My brother Boroto was angry that I wouldn't return. When he'd helped Tomagugu save me all those years ago, he imagined I'd stay with them forever. He was such a hothead that he thought I was being held against my will.

When Gameema came out to see me on the ship, she kissed my hands and wept. When she kissed the shell necklace I had made for her, I felt my heart might break. She had been so kind to me.

Gameema, Yuri and Sibi and the other women brought mats for sitting on, and grass so that we could weave baskets together while we talked. I had sewn myself a gown from the sailors' handkerchiefs and the women were so full of praise and admiration you would have thought I'd made a ball gown. They brought me all my favourite treats—roasted turtle eggs and yams—in woven baskets. They told how many of them wept for me and I felt a different kind of shame to when the sailors had seen me naked. My Islander family had kept me safe all these years, but as much as I loved them, I did not want to be the ghost girl of the Kaurareg forever.

THE FACTS

TOMAGUGU AND BARBARA THOMPSON/GIOM

Who was Barbara Thompson before she was Giom?

Barbara Thompson/Giom was six years old when her family immigrated to Australia from Scotland in 1837. In 1843, when she was barely 12 years old, Barbara/Giom married a sailor called William Thompson. At that time, girls were allowed to legally marry when they turned 12. William and Barbara/Giom were shipwrecked as they sailed around the Cape York Peninsula.

Barbara/Giom was rescued by three men: Tomagugu, Boroto and Alikia. She spent five years, from 1844 to 1849, living with the Kaurareg Islanders and the Aboriginal people of Far North Queensland on Muralug Island.

Who was Tomagugu?

Tomagugu was not a Kaurareg Islander but was from the mainland of Australia. He was related to the Kaurareg through marriage, as his wife, Sibi, was a Kaurareg Islander and Tomagugu travelled regularly between his mainland home and the islands to visit his friends and his wife's family. The people of the islands and mainland Australia often moved between communities and were closely connected to each other. Tomagugu maintained an interest in protecting Barbara/Giom during her time in the Torres Strait Islands. Barbara/Giom described him as 'her brother and the best man in all the islands'.

Islander men approaching the HMS *Rattlesnake* to trade.

THE FACTS

TOMAGUGU AND BARBARA THOMPSON/GIOM

Who was Barbara/Giom's Islander family?

Tomagugu and Boroto both became like brothers to Barbara/Giom for the rest of her time on Muralug Island. People who were not born on country were considered to be like ghosts with no spiritual connection to the land, so Pequi and his family adopted Barbara/Giom, as they believed she was the returned spirit of their much-loved daughter Gieowma (or Giom for short) who had drowned.

Barbara/Giom learned the languages of the Torres Strait Islands and worked alongside the women in her community. In recounting her time with the Kaurareg, she mentioned the names of many men and women who helped her.

Some of the conversations in Tomagugu and Barbara/Giom's stories are verbatim from Barbara/Giom's firsthand account of her time with the Kaurareg. She really did say to the captain of HMS *Rattlesnake*, 'Sir, I am a Christian and would rather go back to my friends.'

What did they eat?

The Kaurareg loved to hunt turtles, especially female turtles. They cooked the turtles and roasted turtle eggs in ground ovens, using layers of pandanus leaves and hot stones and then, finally, a cover of sand. They also ate fish, goannas, flying foxes, birds, eggs and many different fruits and nuts. In the wet season, when food was scarce, they would eat edible mangrove sprouts and other tubers, which had to be carefully prepared to remove poison from the roots.

How did Barbara/Giom live among the Kaurareg?

Barbara/Giom helped with gathering yams and caring for small children. She also helped to collect firewood, shellfish and water. She roasted turtle eggs and meat, and mixed yams with turtle oil to make a delicious mash. Sometimes she helped the other women as they wove baskets, mats and made grass skirts and fish traps using the leaves of the pandanus plants. During the wet season, the Kaurareg built a long house of bark and cane and everyone moved out of their own huts into the long house so that they could share everything.

Barbara/Giom described how the fine canoes of the Kaurareg were made: 'They go into the bush and select a large tree and cut it down with axes—axes they get from the ships that pass. When the tree is felled all the people, men women and children, all help to drag it down to the waterside. They make a cut at each end of the log, then chip it all out with axes out of the middle. They don't use fire … some work at the outrigger poles, some at the float. All going on at once.'

THE FACTS

TOMAGUGU AND BARBARA THOMPSON/GIOM

What happened when Barbara/Giom returned to Sydney?

Some people believe that Barbara/Giom remarried, changed her name, and lived to be a very old woman. There is evidence that she may have had a daughter and is, perhaps, buried in Rookwood Cemetery in Sydney. Barbara/Giom told many stories about her time with the Kaurareg to the men on HMS *Rattlesnake* and they wrote about her adventures, as did newspapers in Sydney.

Barbara/Giom always insisted that the Kaurareg had saved her life and treated her well. The general public were more interested in hearing stories about wild and savage cannibals and they quickly lost interest in Barbara/Giom's true stories of Indigenous people's kindness. Once she returned to Sydney, she soon disappeared from public view.

What happened to the people who cared for Barbara/Giom?

Within a few years of Barbara/Giom leaving the islands, the Kaurareg way of life was almost destroyed. A white settlement was built on the eastern tip of Cape York, and almost immediately conflict began. In 1870, many of the Kaurareg were murdered and their camp and canoes wrecked. The settlers who killed them thought—wrongly—that the Kaurareg had murdered the survivors of a shipwreck and were holding the wife and child of the ship's captain hostage.

In the twentieth century, the Kaurareg were taken from their homes and forced to live on other islands. Finally, in 2001, they were granted native title of five islands, including Muralug Island. The remaining Kaurareg Elders continue to fight to preserve their culture and history.

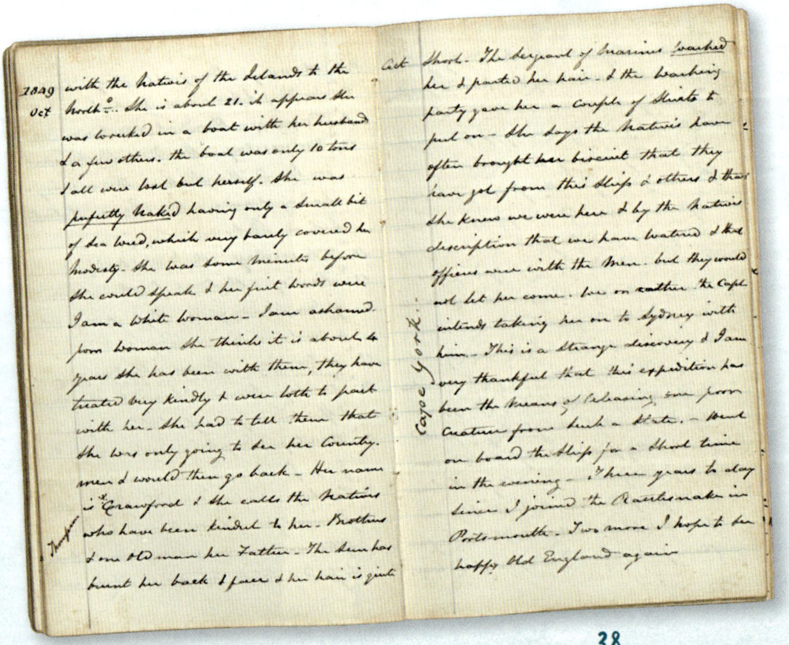

Pages from the diary of George Inskip, second master on the *Rattlesnake*, with a description of Barbara/Giom.

1849, October

'… she calls the Natives who have been kindred to her Brothers & one old man her Father. The sun has burnt her back & face & her hair is quite short. The sergeant of Marines washed her & parted her hair & the washing party gave her a couple of shirts to put on …'

HMS *Rattlesnake*, the ship that took Barbara/Giom back to Sydney, sailing through Sydney Heads.

3

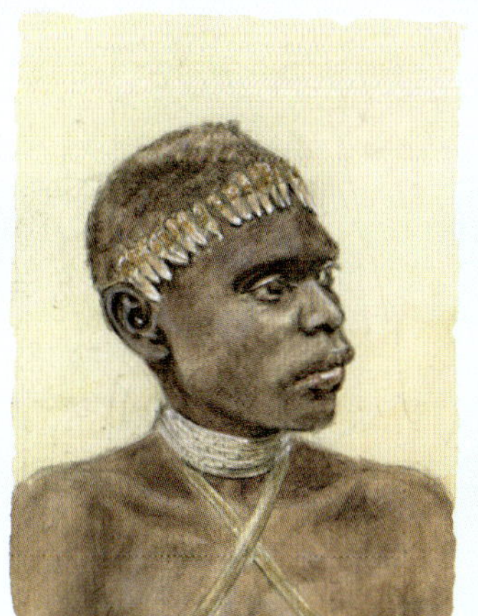

THE BINDAL AND THE SHIPWRECK SURVIVORS

TOWNSVILLE TO BOWEN, 1846–1863

WURRA

'MEN'S BUSINESS TOMORROW, WURRA. BETTER GET SOME SLEEP,' INSTRUCTED MY FATHER.

IT WAS PAST MY BEDTIME. USUALLY THE WAVES LAPPING UPON THE SHORE MADE MY EYELIDS HEAVY, BUT TONIGHT EXCITED CHATTER ABOUT STARS KEPT ME AWAKE.

Shooting stars falling towards the beach meant that something was there, waiting to be found. Whatever waited for us was a mystery, but tomorrow Father and Uncle would take all the young men in the clan on an adventure of discovery.

I was tired the next morning and moved as slowly as a sea cucumber across the seabed. The old men of our tribe and the neighbouring tribe went first, venturing through the trees, heading towards the rocks that jutted out from the waves. Even though it was morning, we remembered the previous night's falling stars and followed their direction.

'Come and see, Wurra,' said Uncle, jumping from foot to foot.

I bounded over rocks and shrubs, as the soil turned into sand. There were four white people all huddled together, scared at the sight of us. They held their hands above their heads—was this their traditional greeting? To calm them, we did the same. When their screams subsided, we lowered our arms and walked towards them. Some of our men gave them food, which they swooped on like seabirds looking for scraps.

I took a deep breath and moved past our old men and right up close to the strangers. Reaching out, I felt the young man's arms, legs and face. He had all the same body parts as me.

'This one's a young man,' I said. 'Like me. That other one is also a man. That little one is a boy and the other, maybe a woman.'

The rest of the old men then came closer and checked the others. I felt important, knowing that they had waited for me to inspect the newcomers first.

'They wear strange skins,' said one man from the other clan, clutching the material that the white lady wore on her back.

At his touch, she screamed and fell on the ground, uttering strange words and crying. The old man helped her up and told her she was safe, but she didn't understand our language.

'We will camp with them,' announced Uncle. 'When the sun rises, we will talk about what to do next.'

The other Elders agreed. We slept well, but I don't think the strangers did. As the sun hit their faces, we realised how weak they were.

'Wurra, these people need food,' instructed Uncle.

I climbed the nearest hill to dig for juicy *moogoondah* root. When we gave it to them, they ate it quickly.

The young man glanced at me, almost gratefully. I smiled back and gave him more *moogoondah* root. He munched on it loudly, just like I do when I have been longing for a snack during a long day of hunting.

After eating time, the old men sat in a circle and yarned. All the Elders had a turn at speaking and there was a lot of agreement.

Two of the Elders from the neighbouring clan pointed to one of the white men and the woman. These two had lain beside each other all night and held one another close. They must have been husband and wife.

'After we return, we will take the couple to live with us,' said one of the old men. 'There is plenty of food to be shared with them and they will be safe.'

'Then we shall take the other man and the boy,' replied Uncle. 'The Bindal will also care for them like we do for our own.'

When the agreement had been made, we celebrated with a corroboree. The white people didn't dance with us, but they did sing a song in their language. It was a slow song, nothing we could shake a leg to.

'Respectful,' murmured Uncle to the other Elders, acknowledging the strangers' song.

The men nodded in agreement.

On the way back to the halfway camp, the strangers were so weak they could barely walk. Uncle picked up the small boy and carried him on his shoulders. I helped the young man of my age, putting his arm about my shoulder and guiding his steps. In my language, I calmly told him that we were nearly there. Of course, he didn't answer, but his body relaxed when he heard my voice. As we neared the camp site, he began to shake at the sight of smoke.

Some of the Elders and our neighbours sat around the flames of the fire, as the smoke wafted high above the trees. They knew we were coming. Their hands were outspread, being warmed by the fire.

'Bring them closer,' they told us.

The four strangers struggled against us, becoming frightened at the sight of the flickering flames. The old men stood and placed their warm palms on the white folk. Instantly, they settled. More food and water were given to them, and preparations were made to take them to our main camp, where they would live as one of the Bindal.

The next day we presented our strange discoveries to the clans—it was both exciting and funny. As wise as our Elders were, they could also be mischievous. Some of our old men dressed in the white people's clothes, then they directed the strangers to lie down and they covered them with dry grass.

When the grass was pulled away, our families were presented with an amazing sight! Some of the women screamed and ran away in fright, others stayed and studied the white people closely. Everyone was surprised. Many of the children cried until their mothers held them to settle their tears.

After our ceremonies, the husband and wife travelled north with the other clan, and the young man and boy lived with us and learned the Bindal ways. The boy was adopted and the man became like a brother to me. Uncle named him Karekynjib-Wombil-Moony.

Most friendships are formed around a camp fire at night, but Karekynjib-Wombil-Moony and I bonded in the early mornings when the wild geese were feeding. I would lead the hunt silently, teaching him to creep through the lowlands as quietly as the breeze the geese flew on.

'Keep up,' I would whisper.

'I'm trying,' he whispered back in language.

As the seasons passed, Karekynjib-Wombil-Moony would meet me as the sun began to float into the morning sky and would soon take the lead with long, silent strides. When we returned, the geese would be shared among the clan. Brother Karekynjib-Wombil-Moony would smile contentedly as he handed them out.

As word spread across the land about the white people found by the shooting stars, tribes from many nations travelled towards our land, just for a glimpse of our new family members. All the tribes gathered, sang and danced for days on end, to celebrate the newcomers. As the celebration ended, we were heartbroken when my new brother ran away with the boy. They had met up with the husband and wife at the celebration, and the four of them headed south to live with another tribe from where the cooler winds blew.

Many moons later, Brother appeared back on Bindal land.

'Wurra!' he called, waiting near the big tree. 'It's me!' he said, remembering our language. He smiled but his eyes looked sad.

'Can I be Bindal again?' he asked.

'That's up to the Elders,' I said, hugging him.

That night, we met with the Elders, including Uncle. They weren't as happy to see him as I was.

'Where are the others?' asked one of our old people.

'They have died,' Brother replied, softly. 'The other clans didn't look after us as well as the Bindal.'

There was a great commotion around the fire and Uncle picked up his spear. 'I should crack you over the head with this!' he shouted. 'They would still be alive if you hadn't run away with them!'

Brother cowered and apologised for his foolishness.

In the end, he was forgiven and allowed to stay. During the years he spent with us, Brother saw babies grow into young men, girls mature into mothers, waves shape the shoreline and fig trees grow taller. Even after all this time, his feet grew itchy again.

White men began invading our lands and murdering our people. As they grew in number, Brother saw it as an opportunity to leave.

One evening, just on dusk, when the smoke from our camp fires was sending the sandflies back to the beach, the Elders called Karekynjib-Wombil-Moony over to them. They had heard him talking about reuniting with the white men who were invading our lands.

'They'll think you're one of us and shoot you dead,' they said.

'I will get clothes and guns from them,' my brother replied. 'I will come back to you.'

But the Elders waved him away. Trouble was brewing.

Two of our old ladies brought news that white men had set up camp at the bottom of a hill called Yamarama.

'Let me visit them and I will ask them to stay away from your land,' said Brother, persuasively.

The next day, we formed a group and travelled to Yamarama.

'Stay in the shadows,' I told my people.

Everyone walked in silence until we reached a place at the top of the hill where we could finally see the white man's hut below. Brother's feet were itchier than ever.

'See you back here soon,' I said. 'We will wait here on Yamarama. Take Yida with you. They won't shoot you if you're with a woman.'

But Brother was already gone, with Yida following close behind. As they reached the foot of the hill, Yida froze at the sight of the white people's curly-haired animals eating grass. Wurra continued on, but Yida fled, her legs pumping back up the hill faster than she had descended.

Our group peered through the trees and down the hill at Brother. Now alone and sitting naked on the fence like a magpie, Brother waited to get the attention of the white men inside. He yelled at them in their language and out they came, guns pointed. They spoke and Brother disappeared inside their hut. Before long, he came climbing back up the hill.

'You have to leave,' he explained. 'There's more of them coming.'

'Will you come with us?' I asked.

'No,' he replied. 'I must keep them away from the Bindal.'

Our people shook their heads. We wanted to believe in him, but everyone knew that the white man was spreading. We were all worried about what this might mean for our people.

Every time I see or hear old man magpie, gargling and calling from the trees, I think of Brother, sitting on the fence that day, knowing that his white feathers were brighter than his black ones. I hope he found his path.

JAMES 'JEMMY' MORRILL

'JEMMY,' SAID CAPTAIN PITKETHLEY. 'GET UP. WE'VE GOT TO KEEP SEARCHING FOR FOOD.'

I SAT UP WEARILY AND LOOKED ABOUT OUR ROUGH CAMP SITE.

The cabin boy was asleep under the shelter of the overhanging rocks and Mrs Pitkethley was huddled beside him, staring forlornly into the bush. We were the last four survivors of the wreck of the *Peruvian* but day by day we inched closer to death.

I struggled to my feet and followed the Captain along the sandy track to the beach, where we scoured the shore for oysters and drank rainwater from rock holes.

Late in the afternoon, when the Captain and I returned to camp empty-handed, we found Mrs Pitkethley weeping.

'We have come to our last now,' she sobbed. 'There are such a lot of wild blacks. They were whistling and jabbering and they are sure to eat us all.'

'Where did you see them?' asked the Captain.

She pointed at a hill in the distance, but all I could see was thick bush and the dark shadows cast by gum trees.

I lay awake all night, terrified by the idea of being eaten by cannibals. When the blacks walked into our camp the next morning, I was sure they would gobble up every piece of me and my companions. We held our hands high in surrender, but the strangest thing happened. The black people raised their hands as if they were surrendering to us!

We persisted in trying to surrender but the blacks kept their hands in the air as well. They seemed afraid of us. Who was surrendering? Them or us?

Eventually, the black men lowered their arms and approached cautiously. They touched our heads and felt our bodies, as if they couldn't quite believe we were human. Then they fed us sweet and nutty root vegetables, more delicious than anything we'd eaten in months.

The next day, using sign language they indicated that they would feed and shelter us if we came away with them. When we nodded that we would, they set about making a dance, and they sang as they danced. I could see they wanted us to join in but how could we sing their strange, tuneless songs? I began to sing 'God Moves in Mysterious Ways', hoping they would like it. It had been one of my favourite hymns when I was a boy. I nodded at the Captain and the others and they joined in too. The song felt right, for to be offered food and comfort from black fellows was a mysterious thing indeed.

After the songs, a strong hunter picked up the cabin boy, who was too weak to walk, and put him on his shoulders. The Captain, his good lady and I were also weak, our feet sore and bleeding. Seeing our distress, the natives helped us on our way. One young man held me steadily, guiding my steps as I struggled to stay upright.

The men led us to a plain where we met three more natives—powerful, serious men who sat around a small fire. I felt a flash of fear as they led us to the fireside. Had we been tricked? Were they going to cook us and eat us after all?

I began to tremble in terror but the men only warmed their hands on the fire and then gently laid them on my face and body, reassuring me that they meant me no harm. They murmured softly and their eyes were kind and my fears melted away.

I never went hungry again. The hill people were skilled hunters. Not only did they catch sharks, snakes, crocodiles, kangaroos and wallabies but they also taught me how to catch and cook grubs, snails and many types of birds. They showed me how to use the bark and root from a particular tree to stun fish and how to make nets and snares for hunting kangaroo and birds.

One of the young hunters, Wurra, became a firm friend to me. He was the same man who had helped me on that very first day when the Bindal people had found me and my companions, starving and wounded. Once I had recovered from my injuries, he often took me hunting and shared his knowledge of the bush and waterways.

The Captain and his wife were sent to live with another branch of the clan, and the cabin boy and I spent nearly six months with Wurra and his people. But when all four of us were reunited at a gathering of the clans, the Captain and I decided we should run away and travel south in hope of finding a British settlement. It was the worst decision we could have made.

THE BINDAL AND THE SHIPWRECK SURVIVORS

It took two years for me to make my way back to the Bindal. One evening after my return, Wurra and I sat together cooking fish on the camp fire. Wurra gazed at me with a puzzled expression and then he asked me about my old life—why had I been so ill and starving when he had first met me? And why had I made the reckless decision to run away?

'I was a sailor on a mighty ship,' I said. 'But it was wrecked on a reef. I clung to a raft, along with some of the other survivors. For more than 40 days and 40 nights we drifted across shark-infested waters.'

'You were with the other three?' he asked.

'Not just the three you met. There were 21 of us to begin with, but some died of starvation. Some of thirst. We grew so desperate that we cut off the leg of a dead sailor and tied it to the end of an oar for bait. On the other oar we secured a snare to catch whatever fish came to eat the severed limb.'

I thought Wurra would be impressed but he simply looked shocked. 'You cut off the leg of your brother to use as bait?'

'He wasn't my brother. Besides, we had to do it. We were starving. And it worked. We caught a shark. What we couldn't eat, we dried in the sun for later. Shark meat kept us alive all those long days before the last of us were washed up on the beach where you found us.'

Wurra shook his head. 'And now all the others are dead.'

I felt a stab of shame, remembering how the Captain, Mrs Pitkethley and the cabin boy had all died when we left the Bindal and tried to make our way south. Shuffling from tribe to tribe, we had grown weary and weak. I put my head in my hands and tried to forget those miserable days.

Wurra put his hand on my shoulder. 'It was good you came home. You are Bindal now.'

As the years passed, it seemed strange to me that I had once wandered through the bush and never realised how much there was to eat in this land of plenty. Wurra taught me how to find breadfruit, native plums, blue, white and red native currants, wild bananas and apples, and red and black figs. Now everywhere I looked I realised that the bush that had seemed so dark and threatening was rich and fertile. It was no surprise that British settlers would come to claim it.

At first I was excited by the arrival of Englishmen on Bindal lands. 'If you see any white fellows, tell them that you have a white man living with you,' I told my Aboriginal brothers.

But when a group of Bindal men tried to explain to some settlers that a white man was living with them, one Bindal Elder was shot dead and another was wounded.

Later, a fishing party of 15 men was killed by settlers for no reason that I could understand. But most shocking was when a white man came upon a funeral and instantly fired his gun. The grieving son who had been embracing the body of his dead father was shot dead. The killing times had begun, and I knew my days with the Bindal would soon come to an end.

When news came of Europeans settling near a place called Yamarama, I begged Wurra to take me there. We travelled south with a small group. Two old women went ahead and came back to report that they had seen the white people's hut.

'You must take a woman with you, Brother,' said Wurra. 'You will always be safer with a woman beside you.'

Halfway down the hill, the woman saw a flock of sheep and took fright. She turned and ran but I refused to go back. At a waterhole near the settler's hut I washed myself, scrubbing every inch of my skin to try and look as much like a white man again as possible.

For a while, I sat at a distance and watched the smoke from the hut's fire drift up into the sky. Then I swallowed my fear and climbed onto the fence so the settlers' barking dog couldn't snap at me. I thought carefully before calling out: 'What cheer, mates?'

Two faces appeared in the door of the hut. I grinned, trying to look friendly, but the next thing I knew they were pointing their guns at my head. I raised my hands and cried, 'Don't shoot me! I am a British object—a shipwrecked sailor.'

As soon as the words left my mouth, I knew I'd spoken nonsense. I was not a British object, I was a British subject.

The two men lowered their guns and gestured for me to approach. Then the interrogation began. They asked me so many questions that I struggled to find words in English.

They offered me bread and sugary tea but the bread stuck in my throat and the sweetness of the tea was disgusting. I could see that they didn't believe my story, no matter how much I tried to explain myself.

'I have to go back and tell my friends that I'm safe,' I told them.

'If you don't come back in the morning, we'll know you're a liar. We'll set the black trackers on to you and they'll shoot the lot of you, you and your lying blackfella friends.'

I walked back up the hill to where the Bindal people waited for me. I knew if I told them that there were only two white men in the hut, they wouldn't be afraid. But they had to be. Two men with guns could slaughter them all.

'Don't go down there,' I said to my clansmen. 'Too many whitefellas. They have come to take your land away.'

'Can you ask these white men to let us keep our ground in the north, to let us fish our rivers? And can we keep the low grounds? We need to harvest water roots there. It's not good land for white people, too near the seacoast and the swamps. Will they let us have that little piece of our own country?'

'I will ask,' I replied. 'But I will have to leave you. If I don't, they will track all of us down and kill us.'

My friends burst into tears and begged me not to leave. The remembrance of their past kindnesses overpowered me. Part of me wanted to stay, part of me wanted to go back to my old life. If I left them, I could do a little good for my dear friends. I might save them yet.

THE FACTS

WURRA AND JAMES 'JEMMY' MORRILL

Who was James 'Jemmy' Morrill?

James 'Jemmy' Morrill was born in England on 20 May 1824, the son of a village engineer. When Jemmy was 16 he became an apprentice sailor and eventually landed in Sydney. In February 1846, he signed on to the *Peruvian*, a ship that was sailing to China. He was 22 years old when the *Peruvian* was shipwrecked near Horseshoe Reef at the southern end of the Great Barrier Reef.

Who was Wurra?

Jemmy did not reveal the names of any of his Aboriginal friends. Wurra is an imaginary character based on the stories Jemmy told about his time with the Bindal clan of the Birri Gubba (or Biri) people.

Who was Jemmy's Aboriginal family?

The first people who took care of Jemmy and nursed him back to health after he was shipwrecked were the Bindal clan. Later he lived with the Juru or Gia (Guya) people of Port Denison before returning to live with the Bindal clan once more. The Bindal clan travelled around the Burdekin River region, but were mostly based around Mount Elliot which was rich in wildlife and edible roots and fruit so that the people never went hungry.

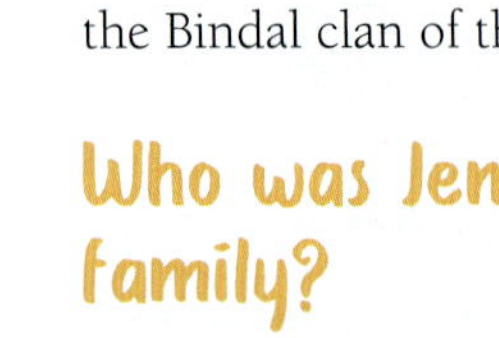

Jemmy in 1863, at the end of his 17 years living with the Aboriginal people of North Queensland.

Townsville and surrounds in the 1870s. The traditional lands of the Birri Gubba clans include the Townsville region.

Breadfruit (above) and cribwood fruit (right).

THE FACTS

WURRA AND
JAMES 'JEMMY' MORRILL

How many years did Jemmy live with the locals?

Jemmy spent a total of 17 years living with Aboriginal people from Mount Elliot to Port Denison, in the Townsville to Bowen area of North Queensland.

Jemmy learned to hunt and fish alongside his Aboriginal friends and became expert at snaring birds. He learned to speak many of the region's languages, and eventually spoke at least eight different dialects. Jemmy never revealed his Aboriginal name but one report suggested that he may have been called Karekynjib-Wombil-Moony.

Why did Jemmy leave?

Jemmy felt torn between wanting to return to live with his own people and remaining with his Aboriginal friends. When the conflict between the settlers and the Aboriginal people over use of the land became more violent, Jemmy believed that he could help the Aboriginal people by negotiating with the invaders. He hoped to persuade the settlers to let the clans keep some of their land and this idea influenced him to finally leave the Bindal.

Jemmy became famous after his return to the white settlements. He argued for land rights for the Aboriginal people who had helped him, but many settlers opposed him.

An Aboriginal Elder of Townsville. Jemmy was heartbroken that his Aboriginal friends were so badly treated by other white men.

What happened when Jemmy returned?

Jemmy was welcomed as a hero when he arrived in Bowen in 1863. People were amazed and impressed that he had survived so many years in the wilderness. He then visited Brisbane to tell his story before returning north. He worked briefly as a negotiator between white settlers and Aboriginal clans, and tried to convince the settlers to grant land rights to the Aboriginal people. Most white people resisted his ideas and the killing of Aboriginal people continued. Jemmy's Aboriginal family felt betrayed by their old friend.

A disappointed man, Jemmy went to work in the customs office in Bowen. Although he married a young servant woman and they had a son, Jemmy did not live long after his return to town life.

Jemmy died in October 1865, at the age of 41, only two years and nine months after returning to live with the British settlers.

What happened to the people who cared for Jemmy?

The Bindal and Juru people suffered terribly in the frontier wars in Queensland. Many were killed or driven from their country. Later, descendants of the Birri Gubba people were removed from their lands and forced to live on missions in other parts of Queensland. Many have since returned to the region, where they continue to live.

This scene was painted in 1802 before the peaceful lives of the Aboriginal people of Bowen were changed forever.

THE KABI KABI AND THE CONVICT

MORETON BAY, 1829–1842

PAMBY-PAMBY

'CAN YOU SMELL IT?' I ASKED MANU.

THE BREEZE BLEW THROUGH HIS HAIR AND ACROSS THE REST OF OUR GROUP, WHO WERE PULLING FISH FROM THEIR NET. THE OTHERS SENSED IT TOO AND SPOKE IN HUSHED TONES SO AS NOT TO SCARE THE WOMEN.

'It's a big animal,' Manu replied, reaching for his spear.

The rest of the men followed his example. I already knew what was approaching, for I had dreamed this moment on many nights. Duramboi was near.

'Put your spears away,' I told them.

'Pamby-Pamby, shouldn't we be ready for danger?' Manu asked.

The others murmured in agreement. They looked upwind, along the banks of the river, ignoring the water hen and searching for other signs of life. That is when he came into view.

'Yeeeow!' screamed the hunters. 'A ghost!'

The figure staggered along the bank, splashing water as he went.

The water hens flew away in fright, and the women and children ran to shelter in the forest. Nearing us, he stopped and fell to his knees.

The men fired questions at him and he answered back. A white man that understood our language! Surely this man should not be feared?

'When you were a black man, what was your name?' asked Manu.

'Who were you before you died?' asked another man.

The newcomer looked around, confused and scared.

'I know who you are,' I told him, pushing through the Kabi Kabi and kneeling down before the white man. I placed my hand on his shoulder. 'I recognise you.'

The men fell silent.

'You are my son, Duramboi,' I said.

The Kabi Kabi began to murmur excitedly among themselves.

'Duramboi's found his way back! Pamby-Pamby's son has returned!' they shouted.

That night was one I will remember forever. We celebrated with dancing and a feast. My son and I were united once again.

It wasn't long before Duramboi was hunting, singing and remembering how to be a Kabi Kabi man. He loved a Kabi Kabi woman and they soon had a son.

One afternoon, many tribes came together to remember the people of a clan that had died not far from our lands.

The white men had tricked them, murdering them with poisoned flour and grains. When it was turned into bread and cooked on the fire, many of our people died after eating it. Families were left without mothers and fathers, children were lost, and hearts were broken.

As we sat around our camp fire the evening before the ceremonies were to begin, a man named Wandi interrupted our gathering to speak with Duramboi. We knew of him. He was a white man, like Duramboi, that had lived with the Carburrah clan. He spent time between them and the white explorers. For a people that had seen so much death at the hands of the white men, we found Wandi very hard to trust.

'Are you Duramboi?' asked Wandi.

Two white men stood behind him. Duramboi said nothing.

Wandi looked as sneaky as a goanna climbing a tree to a bird's nest. 'We've come to take you.'

'I won't go with you!' yelled Duramboi.

Wandi's intentions were as clear as the sneer on his face. He would be rewarded by the white men for bringing in an escaped convict.

Duramboi looked at the two men that Wandi had brought with him. 'I'll go with them, but not you! How could anyone trust a snake like you!'

Wandi tried to argue with Duramboi, but my son told him fiercely, 'My people have seen enough death! If leaving will help protect them, I'll go of my own free will, not as your prisoner.'

Wandi growled and started a war song at Duramboi. But Duramboi had started running away along the riverbank. I knew my life with him was drawing to a close.

When Duramboi returned, he told us of his conversation with the white men down the river.

'They'll kill our people, Father, all of us!' Duramboi cried to me. 'I must leave you.'

I knew he was right. I'd seen enough of our people die—poisoned, murdered and hunted. Enough was enough.

'I will make peace with them, for your sake,' I said, sadly.

This was the second time I would lose my beloved son.

The next morning, Duramboi and I walked to the white men's camp. They were waiting for us, guns by their sides.

'Take this,' I said to them. I held out a white man's treasure. It was shiny and silver and it belonged to one of the poisoners. He died quickly after we found him and punished him for murdering our people.

The white man next to the boat accepted my offering and gave me a new tomahawk, but it meant nothing when I was losing Duramboi.

In his language, the white man told Wandi that he would allow Duramboi to spend one more night with us before they sailed away with him.

I watched Duramboi sleep with his wife and son for most of that evening, resting his body for the last time on our ancient land. As he breathed in and out, I knew that our people's tears would create a new river tomorrow.

As sunlight poked through the leaves of the trees we slept under, the morning air was filled with a terrifying sound.

'Gunshots!' I screamed, but Duramboi placed his hand on my shoulder.

'That's a message from them to me,' explained my son. 'I must leave.'

Our people wouldn't let Duramboi out of their sight. Even as the white men's boat travelled the river, our people followed, walking along the bank.

I tripped and stumbled over the mangroves, my eyes full of tears. Steadying myself, I stood and sang to Duramboi. The rest of our people joined me in song, emerging from their hiding places behind trees and sitting atop branches.

The oars of the white men's boat finally stood still. They drifted on the flat water, as Duramboi took in every verse of my farewell. When our song was finished, I slumped at the base of the mangroves, exhausted.

From the riverbank, I could see Duramboi shaking with emotion. He stood in the boat and replied to me in song.

'I came to you when I was young,' he sang. 'Driven like a dog from the doors of the dead. I told you of all my misery and my torture: I said, 'Do to me as you think best, I am yours', and I dropped as one dead again for I was hungry, thirsty, weak and worn with looking behind me for the hated ones pursuing. You, Pamby-Pamby, you knew me again, could tell who I had been. My father, you took me and you fed me; you gave me water, you gave me meat. I was your son and I was glad. But the great commandant has sent for me. I must go; I will come back. When the moon has come back to you three times, I shall be here.'

His words will haunt me forever.

JAMES 'JEM' DAVIS/DURAMBOI

WHEN I FIRST SAW THE KABI KABI PEOPLE I WAS AFRAID. THEY WERE A MIGHTY GATHERING, 150 POWERFUL BLACK WARRIORS AND THEIR FAMILIES CAMPED ON THE RIVERBANK.

If I hadn't been starving, I might have turned and followed the river back to the beach. But as their voices drifted across the water, I realised that I understood scraps of their language. I'd learned a few phrases from other tribes in the long year that it had taken me to travel to the far north. I decided to take my chances and throw myself on their mercy.

'Who were you before, when you were a black man?' they asked me as I stood among them. 'Who were you before you died?'

I looked from face to face, terrified that I'd be speared for giving a wrong answer. 'It's so long since I died,' I said. 'I can't remember. I've forgotten my name.' It almost felt like the truth.

Once, I'd been a boy called Jem, a blacksmith's son, playing on the streets of Glasgow in Scotland. Then I was James Davis, a 16-year-old thief sent to the other side of the world. Who was I now? A convict on the run, a dead man walking.

A tall, older warrior stepped forward and studied my face. 'Could your name have been Duramboi?' he asked.

'It might have been,' I replied, carefully.

'I recognise you, something in you,' said the man. He touched me gently on my shoulder. 'My son,' he said. 'You are my son, Duramboi.'

He embraced me and everyone began to laugh, as if now that my father had found me, we could all breathe again.

From that day Pamby-Pamby loved me like his blood kin. He was a hunter, a warrior and an Elder of his people and, as the years passed, I grew proud to be his true son.

At night, when we sat around the camp fire together, with the stars bright above us, I tried to tell Pamby-Pamby about Glasgow, about that place a world away where you couldn't see the night sky for the smoke of the city. I tried to tell him of my old life as a convict, too.

'Captain Patrick Logan is the commandant in the south, at Moreton Bay Penal Settlement,' I explained. 'He is the cruellest man you'll ever meet. He treated me like a dog. He'd flog his prisoners for no reason, for the pleasure of hearing us scream.'

'Couldn't your brothers defend you?' asked Pamby-Pamby.

'They were not my brothers. They were the sort of men who'd not think twice about knocking a mate on the head with a pickaxe or slitting his throat while he slept. That's why I ran away. I travelled for seasons and met other tribes in the south before reaching you.'

Pamby-Pamby shook his head. 'I am glad you found your way back to me, Duramboi. Those other lives are behind you now.'

I smiled. I was glad I was no longer Jem Davis. My new name, Duramboi, meant 'kangaroo rat'. Though it had once belonged to Pamby-Pamby's dead son, I felt the name suited me. I grew swift as a hunter and nimble, too. I could climb a tree and gather honey or catch possums as fast as any man of our clan.

Many years of hunting and fishing passed. I fought alongside my brothers, loved my wife and became a father. I was a new man. When my son looked up to me, I was proud to guide him, though I feared for his future. White settlers were slowly moving north, murdering and poisoning the natives as they claimed their lands. The Kabi Kabi fought back but I knew trouble lay ahead for all of us.

Late one evening as we were preparing to meet up with other tribes, I saw a white fellow at a distance, standing in the gathering darkness, talking to my father.

Wandi was the man's name. I knew he was a convict like me who'd been living with Aboriginal people, but I didn't like the look of him. They'd named him Wandi because he never knew when to stop talking. Later, I discovered his English name was David Bracefell. Whatever you called him, he was a shifty fellow. He asked a lot of questions and told my father that the white men who had sailed up the river with him were explorers, not murderers. But I knew Wandi had come to take me back to prison. Convicts often worked for explorers so that their prison sentences were made shorter. If they managed to bring back other runaway convicts, they might even be set free.

On the edge of the camp, two other white men stood waiting. I surrendered to them straight away. I knew it would be better for everyone if I went quickly and peacefully. Wandi was fierce angry with me.

'Why should I surrender to you and let you get the reward? They'll make you a free man for taking me in,' I told him. 'But you know I'll get flogged.'

The other white men couldn't understand us as we argued in language and then Wandi lost his temper and sang a war song at me. It was a terrible, vicious thing to do.

I turned and ran, straight to the camp of white explorers. These men were nothing to me but I knew if they travelled any further, they were doomed and their deaths would bring suffering to the Kabi Kabi. The clans were gathering nearby for ceremonies to commemorate the poisonings of our Aboriginal brothers and sisters at Kilcoy Station. If white men wandered into their midst, our people would take revenge on the invaders. Then there would be more killings and more white men would come to kill my people.

A few English words drifted up through my memory, but when I spoke the words came out wrong and I cursed in the language of my Aboriginal father.

'Stop speaking that black gibberish, man,' said the leader.

In desperation, I tried to make them understand by acting out what had happened to my black brothers, to show how they had died agonising deaths from eating arsenic-laced flour. I clawed the ground with my fingers, tore off my jewellery and rolled on the ground, as if in my death throes. Then I tried to show them how the

shepherds that had poisoned my people were hunted down and punished. When I'd finished, I looked into their faces and realised no one had understood. I think they thought I was mad.

As I slowly recalled some English words, I managed to explain that a shepherd's timepiece, a watch, had found its way into the possession of my father, Pamby-Pamby. They asked me to bring the watch and they would exchange it for a tomahawk.

I promised to return at daybreak. I had no choice.

Pamby-Pamby and the other Elders looked at me as I returned to camp, head down.

'I have to leave you,' I said.

'No, Duramboi. Your life is here, with us,' said Pamby-Pamby.

'Father,' I said, 'remember how I told you about the commandant in the south? I am still a convict. If I don't surrender to these men, they will kill you all. You've seen what they can do with their guns and their poison. I have to leave.'

At sunrise, I heard three musket shots and knew it was time. My life as an Aboriginal man was over. My family clung to me—my son, my wife, my father, all my people embracing me until I felt my heart would break. They kissed me and murmured in low voices, for fear the white men would overhear. Then Pamby-Pamby came with me and presented the explorers with the wretched watch of the murderous shepherds. Trembling, I embraced my father one last time.

No sooner had the oars of the boat dipped into the river, than the bush became alive with my people. They peered from behind the mangroves, afraid of being shot, but their eyes spoke to me. Some climbed onto trees to wave, or emerged from behind rocks. I saw them all—the children, the women, young and old, and my son—reaching out to me.

My father began to sing—a song so sad that it brought tears to my eyes. The others joined in, the whole tribe singing to me across the water. They followed the boat along the river for miles, still singing. I began to shake in every limb and a song rose up in me also, a song for my father who had loved me these past 14 years.

That night, when the explorers camped, I shaved and dressed in white men's clothes.

'You must be glad to have a shirt on your back at last,' said one of my captors.

Every inch of my skin itched from the touch of the fabric. I felt I was shrinking inside. I searched in my memory to find a reply.

'If you had not taken me away,' I said. 'I never would have left them.'

THE FACTS

PAMBY-PAMBY AND JAMES 'JEM' DAVIS/DURAMBOI

Who was James 'Jem' Davis before he became Duramboi?

James 'Jem' Davis/Duramboi was the son of a Glasgow blacksmith. In 1824, when he was 16 years old, he was convicted of theft and sentenced to transportation to Australia for 14 years. Three years after arriving in New South Wales he was punished again for robbery and sent to Moreton Bay Penal Settlement.

Who was Pamby-Pamby?

The explorers who brought Jem/Duramboi back to the penal settlement wrote about meeting Pamby-Pamby who was an Elder and senior warrior of the Kabi Kabi people. Jem/Duramboi described Pamby-Pamby as his father.

Who was Jem/Duramboi's Aboriginal family?

Many of the Kabi Kabi people had never seen a white man before they met Jem/Duramboi. The first tribe that he took shelter with were the Doomgalbarah people near Wide Bay River, 100 miles (160 kilometres) from Moreton Bay Penal Settlement. A year later, Jem/Duramboi travelled north along the coast and then followed the Condamine River inland until he met with a group he called the Gigyabarah clan. These people have been identified as the Kabi Kabi (or Gubbi Gubbi).

Moreton Bay was originally part of New South Wales. Queensland became a separate state of Australia in its own right in 1859.

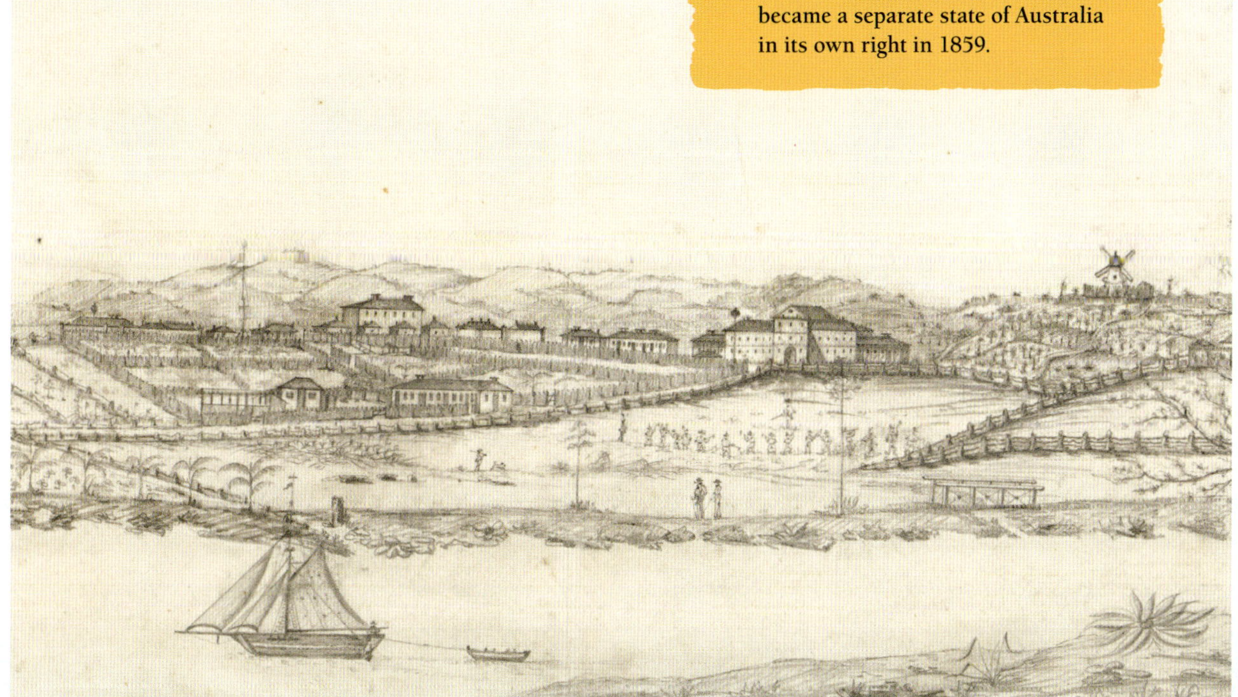

THE FACTS

PAMBY-PAMBY AND JAMES 'JEM' DAVIS/DURAMBOI

How many years did Jem/Duramboi live with the locals?

In February 1829, Jem/Duramboi ran away to live with Aboriginal people. He spent nearly a year travelling north, staying briefly with various Aboriginal people before he was adopted by Pamby-Pamby and renamed Duramboi. In total, he lived with the Aboriginal people of Queensland for nearly 14 years, from 1829 to 1842.

How many other convicts ran away to live with Aboriginal people?

No one knows exactly how many convicts ran away from convict settlements across Australia in the hope of finding a better life with Aboriginal people, but the number may be in the thousands.

In 1823, an escaped convict named Thomas Pamphlett returned to tell stories of his time with the Aboriginal people and inspired many prisoners to run away. Between 1842 and 1844, over 500 of the 2200 prisoners who passed through Moreton Bay Penal Settlement escaped (many of them more than once). Most returned or were caught. Sometimes Aboriginal people handed the convicts back to the authorities, considering runaways to be trespassers on Aboriginal land. But some convicts, like Jem/Duramboi, were loved by Aboriginal people as family. David Bracefell was also adopted into a tribe as a runaway convict. His Aboriginal name was Wandi, which means 'great talker'.

What was the Kilcoy massacre?

Kilcoy sheep station was not far from the southern end of the Bunya lands. In 1842, shepherds working on the station gave sacks of arsenic-laced flour to the Aboriginal people in the area. Fifty to 60 men, women and children used the flour to cook damper and were poisoned. They died horrible, agonising deaths. The poisonings triggered a frontier war in Queensland between Aboriginal people and the invading settlers.

An Aboriginal man of the Kabi Kabi people holding a club and boomerang.

The Kabi Kabi people taught Jem/Duramboi to swiftly climb tall trees using a vine. In later times, they used rope.

THE FACTS

PAMBY-PAMBY AND JAMES 'JEM' DAVIS/DURAMBOI

After his return, Jem/Duramboi opened a crockery shop in George Street, Brisbane.

What happened when Jem/Duramboi returned?

When Jem/Duramboi first returned, the authorities forced him to act as a guide while he served the rest of his prison sentence. In 1844, two years after his return, he was granted his ticket of leave to work for others or for himself.

Jem/Duramboi set up a blacksmith shop at Kangaroo Point, and later moved to Brisbane and opened a crockery shop. He married twice. His first English wife was called Annie, his second was Bridget Hayes. At one stage, he arranged for his Aboriginal son to come and live with him in Brisbane but it's believed his new wife drove the boy away. It is not clear whether it was Annie or Bridget who rejected his Aboriginal son.

Jem/Duramboi also acted as an interpreter for Aboriginal people in the courts from the 1850s through to the 1880s. As he grew older he became very grumpy with people who asked him about his Aboriginal life. When a journalist visited his shop and offered him money for his story he said: 'Do you see the door there? Well, the sooner you get out of my shop the better and if you want any information about the blacks, take your clothes off and go and live with them as I did.'

Jem/Duramboi died in 1889 following a bad beating by his last wife, Bridget Hayes.

A group of Kabi Kabi people of Queensland waiting to begin a ceremony. This photo was taken at the start of the twentieth century, more than 40 years after Jem/Duramboi lived with the Kabi Kabi.

Jem/Duramboi was described as 'a grumpy old man' by people who tried to interview him. He refused to talk about his life with the Kabi Kabi.

What happened to the people who cared for Jem/Duramboi?

After the Kilcoy poisonings, the frontier war between new settlers and the Aboriginal people of Queensland became increasingly violent and many of the Kabi Kabi were murdered or driven from their lands.

Although it is believed Jem/Duramboi returned to visit his Aboriginal family on several occasions, he became very bitter over time and refused to discuss his Aboriginal life.

5

THE MER ISLANDERS AND THE LOST BOYS

TORRES STRAIT, 1834–1836

PANNEY

'PANNEY! HAVE YOU HEARD THE NEWS?' CRIED DUPPA.

MY HUSBAND WAS BIGGER THAN MOST OF THE MEN ON OUR ISLAND. HIS CANOE ROCKED TO THE SIDE AS HE SWUNG HIS STRONG LEGS OUT OF THE BOAT AND WALKED UP THE SAND TO REACH ME.

Our elder son, Bowdoo, a strong man himself, ran up the beach, respectfully staying behind Duppa.

'Is it about the two white boys on Sirreb Island?' I asked.

Word travelled fast on the water. Some of Duppa's fishing party, mainly the young ones, had already reached the shore. Old man Oby broke the news to me and was very excited. He told me that the white boys had been treated poorly and were still being held captive by the Gam le Islanders. Duppa didn't say much to this, only aiming a concerned grunt in the direction of Sirreb Island. He looked at the tide, and at the first stars appearing with dusk.

'Oby's right,' he finally said. 'The white boys saw their people killed right in front of them.'

'We must find these poor children,' I gasped.

'One is nearly old enough to fend for himself,' replied Duppa. 'The other only an infant.'

I looked at our son Bowdoo, and then cast my eyes down to the water's edge where his own little ones played. I smiled to myself, knowing that we had raised our children into strong adults. My arms longed for the embrace of another child, but I was too old to have another of my own.

That night, the flames from the fire illuminated my grandchildren as I held them close to my breast. Old Oby was getting ready to tell stories, but the only story people wanted to hear was about the two mysterious white boys, stranded on Sirreb Island.

So Oby began with the tale that he had told me earlier, but this was old news now. Our people, the Mer Islanders, wanted to know more: where had the white boys come from, and who were they? Many of the women were worried about the youngest child not having a mother or father to care for him.

'I will care for them,' I said, quietly.

The flames flickered and people continued to speak. My grandchildren wriggled around in my arms. The only soul who heard me was Duppa. He broke off his conversation with the men and cast me a puzzled look.

'I will care for them!' I announced, more forcefully.

This time the voices fell silent.

'My wife is speaking,' Duppa said, proudly. This was his way of telling our people to listen. They did as they were told.

'The boys on Sirreb are without their own kind,' I said, passing the grandchildren to my daughter-in-law. 'If they have no one, then I will love them. Duppa too. Just like our own.'

Everyone spoke in hushed tones. They thought I couldn't hear them, but I could. Some worried that if we took the boys, war might start between the islands. Others agreed.

Wise Oby calmed everyone. 'Panney is right,' he said. 'If anyone can care for them it is Panney and Duppa.' He turned to Duppa. 'When is the best tide to travel to Sirreb?'

Duppa considered this question for a moment, but I decided for him.

'Tomorrow, before the sun rises,' I said. 'I will be holding those boys when we return home.'

Everyone looked at Duppa, awaiting his response. But what could he say? All he needed to do was get the canoe ready.

The Sirreb and Gam le Islanders met us as our canoe touched the sand. The war between our islands had long since finished, but they treated Duppa with a healthy amount of fear and respect.

'I have these bananas for you,' smiled Duppa. He held out two big branches of bananas.

We scanned the area for any signs of the two boys. I spotted them peering out from behind one of their houses. One was a tall, thin, dark-haired child who was almost a young man; the other, a tiny fair-haired boy. I patted Duppa on the arm and looked in the direction of the two white faces. He nodded at me, having already seen them.

'And I would like to take the two boys in return,' he said, pointing towards the children.

The man he was bartering with looked shocked but, knowing better than to argue with Duppa, he agreed.

My feet moved like lightning over the grass towards the boys. Their two faces were still and terrified. Knowing better than to frighten them more, I stopped just before reaching them.

'My name is Panney,' I smiled. 'You are safe with me and Duppa.'

The eldest one came forward, speaking some of our language. He introduced himself as Waki and the youngest as Uass. He held the hand of Uass and told him not to be scared.

On the journey home, Waki impressed Duppa by taking a paddle and working at the front of the boat. I held little Uass all the way home, just as I said I would. The boy snuggled in tight and slept under the shade of a grass mat that I held over him. His skin felt as soft as my own grandchildren's. Despite his baby features, his face was tired. I held him tighter.

The welcoming party awoke Uass from his sleep. Song and smoke reached us on the warm salty sea breeze and the celebrations began.

Waki and Uass were now Mer Islanders and my children. Our people ran their fingers through the fine hair of our new sons.

As their hair grew longer and their skin darker, something in my heart knew that

Waki, the older boy, longed for something else. Something that I was unable to give him.

I sat near him, watching him tend to his yam patch and banana trees. Oby was close by, playing with little Uass.

'I see you watching them,' I said to Waki.

The boy looked up from his garden. 'Watching what, Mother?'

'You don't need to hide it, my son,' I said. 'The big boats. The white men's boats. You wish to be with them.'

Waki didn't answer. He didn't need to. My heart sank and I knew Duppa would also grieve if we were to lose this boy.

It wasn't long before another big boat appeared on the horizon. The white sails that caught the wind brought it closer to the beach. Its men came ashore in smaller boats. Our men surrounded the white sailors, offering them tortoise shells and coconuts, ready to trade for axes and other tools. One of the white men spoke some of our language. He hopped out of his boat, his moon-white feet submerged in the shallows.

'No trade, not until we see the white boys,' he demanded.

Duppa looked back towards the beach, hoping that Waki was nowhere to be seen. In our hut, I held Waki tightly, begging him not to go, but he broke free. He ran to the beach and stood next to his adoptive father, allowing himself to be seen by the white boatman.

'They will steal you,' said Duppa, panicking. 'You must not go!'

Waki held Duppa by the shoulders. A tear fell down his now tanned cheek.

'Tell Mother I love her,' said Waki. 'But Uass and I have to go back to our people across the sea.'

Duppa knew this was the beginning of the end. He fetched old man Oby and travelled with Waki out to the big boat. That night while both men slept on the boat either side of Waki, I lay in our hut, holding Uass. He slept soundly as I listened to his every breath.

The next morning, I was awoken by the strange sight of Waki walking towards our hut wearing white men's clothes. He was crying uncontrollably and apologising to me as he approached.

'I am sorry, Mother. I must take Uass,' Waki sobbed.

I cried for Waki to stop, but he took Uass in his arms, clutching him tightly. Uass woke, screaming in fright. He reached out for me as Waki, still sobbing, carried my little boy down to the beach. The white men from the big boat waited.

'Allow me to hold him one more time,' I pleaded. 'Let me take him to the big boat.'

Waki handed Uass to me and I savoured every second—every paddle stroke and every wave that passed beneath us—until we arrived alongside the white men's boat.

As the sailors reached down to take Uass from me, his screams grew louder and his grip became tighter. Uass would not let go.

Waki whispered in his ear. 'Uass, you're upsetting Mother. Please stop crying.' He took the small boy in his arms.

PANNEY

By the time Uass had settled, arrangements had been made for our boys to visit the island one more time, before leaving us and sailing away with the white men.

Duppa sent forward a message to the island that Waki and Uass were leaving. Our people crowded the shore, showering the boys with kisses, hugs and gifts of food, until the canoe sat low in the water under the great weight of coconuts, yams and bananas.

My husband's eyes were now wet with tears. He broke through the crowd to embrace Waki one last time.

The big boat sailed away from the shore and our cries and songs filled the afternoon air, drifting towards the rising moon.

We had made Waki and Uass promise to return, but Duppa and I knew we'd only see our boys through the stars in the night sky.

JOHN IRELAND/WAKI AND WILLIAM D'OYLEY/UASS

MY TRUE NAME WAS JOHN IRELAND. BUT IN 1834, ON SIRREB ISLAND, I WAS RENAMED WAKI AND MY TINY COMPANION, LITTLE WILLIAM D'OYLEY, BECAME UASS.

I was 15 and he was barely three years old. He was the son of a captain and I was only a cabin boy, but we were bound together through tragedy.

We'd been captives of the Gam le Islanders for four months and taken by canoe from one island to the next, as if we were baggage. Uass had begun to babble in the language of the Islanders. Even when I spoke to him in English, he would answer with a muddle of two languages. He rarely cried for his mama any more.

One bright morning, a group of Islanders arrived to trade with our captors. A man called Duppa and his wife, Panney, climbed out of a long canoe.

Panney smiled at us and picked up Uass, holding him gently. 'We heard of you boys from our friends on Erub Island,' she whispered to me. 'We have come to rescue you.'

'I'll give you two branches of bananas for the white boys,' said Duppa.

Our captors looked sour. Two branches of bananas was not a good price, but I could tell they were a little afraid of Duppa. He was a tall and powerfully built warrior. Some of the Islanders who had treated us badly muttered angrily, but now we were to become Panney and Duppa's boys and no one dared harm us. Within hours, we were seated safely in Duppa's beautiful long canoe, gliding across the sea.

On Mer Island we were welcomed with a celebration and a feast. Though Duppa and Panney already had five grown-up children, they treated us as their own. Duppa gave me a piece of land to farm and taught me how to grow yams, coconuts and bananas. He gave me a bow and arrow and took me hunting with his other sons, teaching me how to nock the arrow in place and shoot straight and true. Then one day, he led me down to the beach to admire a brand new canoe. Duppa had arranged for it to be sailed to Mer Island from New Guinea.

'It's a beauty,' I said, as I ran my hand along the edge of the craft.

'It's yours, my son,' said Duppa.

'Mine?'

No one had ever given me anything so beautiful. It was 60-feet long with two masts and a wide sail that extended between them, the sort of canoe that could glide through the water like a dolphin.

'Thank you, Father,' I said, almost breathless with excitement.

Duppa smiled and together we launched the canoe into the sparkling turquoise sea.

Little Uass grew plump now that he could eat to his heart's content. Every day we feasted on yams, sweet potatoes, bananas, fresh cooked fish and coconut milk. One morning, I watched Uass run down to the beach with the other children and noticed how strong and sturdy his limbs had grown. He threw back his head and laughed as he splashed in the shallows with his playmates. He had grown so tanned that only his fair hair made him recognisable as a white child.

Old grandfather Oby took special care of Uass and soon the little boy was speaking the language of the Mer Islanders as if he knew no other. But there were nights when Uass would cry and I was the only one who could calm him. Though we no longer spoke English together, I would lie down beside him and speak softly until he nodded off to sleep.

'He had another nightmare,' said Oby. 'But he will not tell me what he dreamed.'

'Perhaps he is remembering things no boy should remember,' I said, as we watched Uass sleeping.

Old Oby frowned. 'What happened, Waki?'

'I wasn't there when they murdered his parents,' I whispered, bitterly. 'His father was a captain and his mother was a good lady. He had a brother too, called George.'

'Were these people your family also?' asked Oby.

'No,' I replied. 'I was a cabin boy, hired to work on a great ship that sailed from England. Uass and his family were travelling on that ship but it was smashed to pieces on a reef. We were all shipwrecked.'

'Perhaps his family drowned,' said Oby, avoiding my gaze as he looked down at Uass.

'Oby, I saw them kill the other sailors that survived with me. I saw them cut their heads off and do unspeakable things to their bodies.'

I could barely bring myself to tell Oby what I'd seen those natives do to the living and the dead while Uass lay beside us. 'Uass had an older brother, George. He told me their parents were horribly murdered. He said that his mama was holding little Uass tight and screaming. Uass was only saved because some Islander women rushed forward and snatched him away before the warriors could murder him. Only four of us survived the massacre, four boys and the ship's dog. Not a single adult was allowed to live. I don't even know what's happened to George and the other cabin boy.
I hope Uass will forget everything he saw, but I can never forget.'

Old Oby shook his head and then lay down on the other side of Uass. Gently, he stroked the sleeping boy's golden hair. If Uass were to wake again, he would find us both beside him, protecting him from harm.

Panney and Duppa understood that I wanted to go back to my own people but whenever a ship came to trade, they told me I wouldn't be safe with such dangerous men. Sometimes they would keep Uass and me away from the shore so the sailors couldn't see us. Other times, Duppa rubbed black paint onto my skin and painted a red stripe across my face while Panney and my island sisters put ornaments around my neck and fussed over me, threading tasselled grass earrings in my ears so no one would believe I was a white boy.

One day, from atop a high hill I saw the white sail of a ship approaching on the horizon. My heart leapt. I still longed to return to my family in England.

The Islanders took tortoise shell and coconuts down to the beach, hoping to exchange them for iron and axes with the sailors. But they came back disappointed.

'The captain of the ship said nothing will be traded until we take Waki to him.'

'Me! They've come for me!' I cried, unable to hide my excitement.

'It's not safe,' said Panney. 'What if they steal you away?'

'I won't leave,' I said. 'I'll only get some axes for us.'

On board the *Isabella*, the captain gave me clothes and a straw hat and offered me beer. A sailor set a plate of bread and cheese before me. I stared at the food but couldn't touch it. After two years of living as an Islander, my English words had slipped away from me and I struggled to make myself understood.

That night, Duppa and Oby came on board and slept either side of me, to make sure the men of the *Isabella* meant me no harm.

The next day, the captain insisted that Uass be brought on board too.

'Tell them he is crying,' said Duppa. 'Or that he is asleep. Tell them he will not leave the women.'

'But, Father, we have to go back to our own people.'

Reluctantly, Duppa instructed some men to fetch him. Uass screamed as the sailors tried to lift him from the canoe and he clung tightly to Panney. I climbed down and put my head next to his fair curls. I whispered to him until his screams subsided. Finally, Uass let me take him from Panney. Her face was stricken as the canoe took her back to shore.

When the sailors dressed Uass, he pulled at his new clothing and threw his cap on the deck. I knew how he felt. I'd forgotten how irritating a collar could feel.

In broken English, I told the captain that our Mer Island family had treated us well and that I owed my life to my father, Duppa. I convinced the captain to reward Duppa, Panney and Oby with many gifts. Yet when we had to part, both Duppa and Oby were miserable.

'Only come and say goodbye to your mother and brothers and sisters one last time,' begged Duppa.

More than 100 Islanders gathered on the beach. They hugged us and covered little Uass with kisses. Duppa brought a basket full to the brim with coconuts and yams and loaded it into the boat.

'For you, and for Uass,' he said. Then he put his strong arms around me. 'Who is to care for your canoe and your bow and arrow when you are gone?' he asked, his eyes filling with tears.

I hugged him tightly. 'Give them to my brother, Bowdoo,' I said.

Duppa nodded and rested his cheek against mine. I will never forget his last words to me.

'Come back to us soon, my son. Do not forget your island home.'

THE FACTS

PANNEY AND JOHN IRELAND/WAKI AND WILLIAM D'OYLEY/UASS

Who were John Ireland and William D'Oyley before they became Waki and Uass?

In 1834, John Ireland/Waki was a tall, thin 15-year-old cabin boy from one of London's outlying villages. He first joined the crew of the *Charles Eaton* on the ship's voyage from England to Australia. William D'Oyley/Uass was three years old when the *Charles Eaton* was shipwrecked in the Torres Strait. His father, Captain Thomas D'Oyley, was an officer in a British regiment. William/Uass' mother, Charlotte, eight-year-old brother, George, and their Indian nursemaid, were all travelling from Hobart to Indonesia.

Who was Panney?

Panney was an Elder of the Mer Islanders. Her husband, Duppa, was also a respected Elder of their clan. At the time of adopting the two shipwrecked boys, the couple already had grown-up children—three sons and two daughters—and many grandchildren.

Duppa, John/Waki and William/Uass' Islander father is pictured sitting with an axe in his hand. Duppa's grown-up son (also called Duppa) is standing holding a spear beside his wife, Areg.

THE FACTS

PANNEY AND JOHN IRELAND/WAKI AND WILLIAM D'OYLEY/UASS

Why were the shipwrecked adults killed?

The Gam le Islanders, who first encountered the shipwrecked survivors of the *Charles Eaton*, thought adult Europeans were violent and dangerous. Torres Strait Islanders had witnessed the deaths of their own people who had been shot and killed by Europeans, so some Islanders considered white people their enemies. The two cabin boys, John Ireland/Waki and John Sexton, and the young D'Oyley brothers were not killed because they were children and too young to be a threat.

How did John/Waki and William/Uass live among the Islanders?

John/Waki was given his own land and canoe. He had his ears pierced and joined in some of the Islander ceremonies. He also learned to speak the language of the Mer Islanders. Duppa taught John/Waki to hunt and fish and how to use a bow and arrow.

William/Uass quickly adjusted to his new home on Mer Island. Oby, a neighbour of Duppa and Panney, treated Uass as his favourite grandson. Panney is only mentioned briefly in firsthand accounts but Uass was described as being distressed at having to leave his Islander family.

John/Waki and William/Uass lived with the Islanders of the Torres Strait for nearly two years from 1834 to 1836.

Funeral rites

Long ago, when Islanders were at war, they would sometimes cut off the heads of their enemies and take the severed heads back to their island for ceremonies. During the ceremony, they would sometimes cut small pieces of flesh from the bodies of their enemies and eat them. They believed this meant that they took on the strength of the warriors that they had killed in battle. This funeral rite is called 'ritual anthropophagy' and is not the same as cannibalism, where people eat other people in hunger.

The skulls of captured enemies were used in rituals and ceremonies. This picture appeared in a book written later by John Ireland.

An Islander outrigger setting out to meet ships for trade.

THE FACTS

PANNEY AND JOHN IRELAND/WAKI AND WILLIAM D'OYLEY/UASS

What happened when John/Waki and William/Uass returned?

The *Isabella* searched some of the other Torres Strait islands for more survivors of the wreck of the *Charles Eaton* but none were found. George D'Oyley had died of illness and the other cabin boy, John Sexton, died of a spear wound.

John/Waki and William/Uass were taken to Sydney. After several months there, John/Waki returned to England alone. He had been away from his London home for four years. In 1845, when he was 26 years old, he published a book about his adventures entitled *The Shipwrecked Orphans*.

On arrival in Sydney, four-year-old William/Uass could no longer speak English. One account says that the captain of the *Isabella* took him straight back to England. Another states that a friend of the D'Oyley family, Mrs Slade of Sydney, claimed him. It is said that when he hugged Mrs Slade for the first time he called her 'Mamma', the only English word that he could remember.

These pictures appeared in John Ireland's book, *The Shipwrecked Orphans*.

Mer Islanders used fiery torches to attract fish when night fishing.

Duppa taught John/Waki to use a bow and arrow.

John/Waki showed Duppa how to use heat from a fire to soften and shape iron.

An oil painting of William/Uass being taken out to the *Isabella*. In reality, he cried and clung to his Islander mother.

What happened to the people who had cared for John/Waki and William/Uass?

For more than a century after John/Waki and William/Uass left the islands, the Islanders of the Torres Strait suffered badly at the hands of the British and Australian people. In 1992, after a long struggle in the Australian courts, Meriam man Eddie Koiki Mabo, along with four other people, achieved recognition that the Indigenous people of the Torres Strait Islands had the right to control their own land and should never have been deprived of that right by the British and Australian governments. The Mabo decision is a landmark in Australian history.

Erub and Meriam islanders often wore elaborate masks when performing ceremonial dances.

anthropophagy the culture and practice of eating human flesh in a ritual context

arsenic a naturally occurring element whose compounds can be used as a lethal poison, often as a pesticide

blacksmith a craftsman who creates and repairs iron objects, such as horseshoes, using heat to soften the metal

dialect form of a language unique to a specific region or group

dugong a large marine mammal, sometimes called a sea cow, that lives in warm coastal waters; it feeds only on seagrass

exorcise to cast out or drive away evil spirits by a ceremony, such as prayer

frontier war brutal conflict between Indigenous people and white settlers during the period of British colonisation of Australia

Indigenous native or original to a region; in Australia, Indigenous groups are the Aboriginal and Torres Strait Islander people who occupied the continent prior to British settlement

mangroves trees or shrubs of tidal, coastal swamps with many roots protruding above the mud

marki Kaurareg word for 'ghost'. Used to refer to white people as they were thought to be like ghosts who had no spiritual connection to country.

mère French word for 'mother'

mission an establishment set up by churches during the nineteenth century to house and 'Christianise' Indigenous peoples, and prepare them to work for the settlers

moogoondah root the root of a type of native rosella, a shrub that is a member of the hibiscus family. Its roots, leaves, shoots and seedpods are edible. *Moogoondah* may have been Jemmy's interpretation of the Wulguru word *mayulumu*.

muungkal (wongai plums) fruit of the wongai tree, similar in taste and texture to a date

negotiator a person who helps bring about an agreement between two or more groups by talking to each of them

nock to fit an arrow in place on a bowstring, ready for shooting; the notch in a bow for holding the arrow in place

pandanus palm-like tree or shrub of the tropics and subtropics; provides food and materials for housing, clothing and textiles

penal settlement isolated colony established to separate convicts from society as a punishment; often treatment of convicts was brutal

père French word for 'father'

ticket of leave a document of parole or early release issued to convicts who had shown they could be trusted with some freedoms, such as working, marrying and owning property

toomah a way of saying 'tomorrow' in pidgin English, but used to imply 'soon' or 'in a little while'

tuber a vegetable that grows underground on the stem of a plant, such as potatoes or yams

NOTES ON SOURCES

Strangers on Country is largely based on a book for adults entitled *Living with the Locals: Early Europeans' Experience of Indigenous Life* by John Maynard and Victoria Haskins. John and Victoria are historians based at the University of Newcastle in NSW and they spent many years researching the stories of the castaways and convicts who found refuge with Indigenous people.

Living with the Locals includes the stories of nine Europeans and the people who cared for them in NSW, Victoria and Queensland. We chose to focus on five of these stories, all set in Queensland and the Torres Strait, in part because these stories featured younger characters but also because Dave could relate to stories set around his traditional country. Kirsty enjoyed doing additional research into the lives of these particular castaways and convicts.

Hundreds of convicts ran away from penal settlements in the hope of finding a home with Aboriginal people. No one knows exactly how many shipwrecked men, women and children sought refuge with Aboriginal people in the days when sailing was the only way to reach Australia. Many castaways and convicts never returned to town life but the stories of those who did, including the ones in this book, appear in historical records.

The names of the white settlers and convicts that were recorded through time are accurate. The names of the Aboriginal and Torres Strait Islander characters are as they appear in the records. In a few instances in this book, an Indigenous character's name has been added by the authors. This was necessary because early records did not always include the names of the Aboriginal or Torres Strait Islander people involved. Sadly, the names of our First Peoples weren't important to the majority of white Australians.

When writing Wurra and James 'Jemmy' Morrill's story, we could find little mention of specific Aboriginal people and names in the historical records. To honour the Bindal, the strength of their people and the way they cared for James Morrill, we consulted language lists of the Townsville to Bowen area to find an appropriate name for Wurra. Wurra means 'grey kangaroo' in the Biri language which was spoken by the Bindal and many of the clans in the Cape Cleveland area where Jemmy was shipwrecked.

Across all stories, we used creative licence and our deepest respect to bring the Indigenous and non-Indigenous characters to life. It is also important to note that we have used our own interpretation of the gathered research to shape the stories, and our imaginations to recreate the voices and thoughts of the characters. In each story, we included as many verbatim quotes from the original sources as possible. Sometimes these sources include words written to describe Indigenous Australians that are not used today.

Sadly, much traditional Aboriginal knowledge was ignored and destroyed at the time of invasion. These stories reveal that many Indigenous people were ready to embrace outsiders, as long as the newcomers respected their laws and customs. The castaways and convicts featured in these stories learned the language and traditions of their host families. The evidence shows that the castaways and convicts grew to admire the rich cultural life of their hosts. When they returned to live among white people, they spoke fondly of the people who had rescued them and were reluctant to reveal sacred traditions and, for the most part, kept faith with the communities that had cared for them.

The use of Aboriginal clan, group or language group names in this book is not authoritative or definitive in terms of history or location. Wherever possible, the names used for the clans or groups have been taken directly from original historical materials, as researched by John Maynard and Victoria Haskins. In many instances, these historical papers offer varied and misspelt Aboriginal group names, depending on who originally wrote them down in the nineteenth century. When present-day names of Aboriginal groups are mentioned, we followed John and Victoria's use of the Australian Institute of Aboriginal and Torres Strait Islander Studies (AIATSIS) reference names.

Dave Hartley and Kirsty Murray

LIST OF ILLUSTRATIONS

Note: the titles of some of these images, which reflect the creator's attitude or that of the period in which the image was created, may be considered inappropriate today.

LIST OF ILLUSTRATIONS

LIST OF ILLUSTRATIONS

Note: the titles of some of these images, which reflect the creator's attitude or that of the period in which the image was created, may be considered inappropriate today.

LIST OF ILLUSTRATIONS

NOTE FROM THE ILLUSTRATOR DUB LEFFLER:

These stories have a romanticism about them, yet they are all true! Illustrating them meant they needed to be grounded in historical reality but they also needed a certain 'living' quality—as if we were watching the stories unfold in real-time. While I used as many photographs for reference as I could, there are some imaginative embellishments—if only to imbue the characters with a sense of living history.

INDEX

INDEX

F

G

H

I

J

K

L

M

INDEX

ACKNOWLEDGEMENTS

The stories in *Strangers on Country* are largely based on information found in *Living with the Locals* by John Maynard and Victoria Haskins, published by the National Library of Australia. We are grateful to John and Victoria for their meticulous work and for providing us with so much detailed information to draw upon. Although we also used other sources to understand the times in which the characters lived, we always referred to *Living with the Locals* to ensure the stories accurately reflected our principal source of information.

We are grateful to Susan Hall of the National Library of Australia for commissioning us to write *Strangers on Country*, for bringing us together, and for encouraging and challenging us to make the stories vivid and accessible to young readers. We also thank Irma Gold for her attention to detail and excellent editing of a complex manuscript. We owe thanks to Chris Evers for his brilliant advice on Indigenous use of plants, and for pointing us in the direction of Angela Terrill's lexicon of the Biri language.

We acknowledge the traditional Indigenous peoples that appear in the stories in this book and all their descendants of today. We pay our deepest respects to the many families who so generously cared for and often saved the lives of strangers who arrived unexpectedly in their homes. We honour their memory, their kindness and their ongoing connection to country.

Dave Hartley and Kirsty Murray